KV-033-163

DONCASTER LIBRARY SERVICE

30122 03085513 0

CROCODILE CREEK: 24-HOUR RESCUE

A cutting-edge medical centre.
Fully equipped for saving lives and loves!

**Crocodile Creek's state-of-the-art Medical
Centre and Rescue Response Unit is home to a
team of expertly trained medical professionals.
These dedicated men and women face the
challenges of life, love and medicine every day!**

An abandoned baby!

The tension is mounting as a new-born baby
is found in the Outback whilst a young girl
fights for her life.

Two feuding families!

A long-held rivalry is threatening the well-being
of the community. Only hospital head
Charles Wetherby holds the key to this bitter battle.

A race to save lives!

Crocodile Creek's highly skilled medical rescue
team must compete with the fierce heat of the
Australian Outback and the scorching power
of their own emotions.

Meredith Webber says of herself, 'Some ten years ago, I read an article which suggested that Mills and Boon were looking for new medical authors. I had one of those "I can do that" moments, and gave it a try. What began as a challenge has become an obsession, though I do temper the "butt on seat" career of writing with dirty but healthy outdoor pursuits, fossicking through the Australian Outback in search of gold or opals. Having had some success in all of these endeavours, I now consider I've found the perfect lifestyle.'

Recent titles by the same author:

SHEIKH SURGEON
COMING HOME FOR CHRISTMAS
THE ITALIAN SURGEON*
THE HEART SURGEON'S PROPOSAL*
THE CHILDREN'S HEART SURGEON*

Jimmie's Children's Unit

THE DOCTOR'S MARRIAGE WISH

BY
MEREDITH WEBBER

MILLS & BOON

All the characters in this book have no existence outside the imagination
of the author, and have no relation whatsoever to anyone bearing the
same name or names. They are not even distantly inspired by any
individual known or unknown to the author, and all the incidents are
pure invention.

All Rights Reserved including the right of reproduction in whole or in
part in any form. This edition is published by arrangement with
Harlequin Enterprises II B.V. The text of this publication or any part
thereof may not be reproduced or transmitted in any form or by any
means, electronic or mechanical, including photocopying, recording,
storage in an information retrieval system, or otherwise, without the
written permission of the publisher.

MILLS & BOON and MILLS & BOON with the Rose Device
are registered trademarks of the publisher.

First published in Great Britain 2006
Harlequin Mills & Boon Limited,
Eton House, 18-24 Paradise Road, Richmond, Surrey TW9 1SR

© Meredith Webber 2006

ISBN 0 263 19084 6

DONCASTER LIBRARY AND INFORMATION SERVICE	
30122030855130	
Bertrams	15.04.06
	£12.25

Set in Times Roman 10¼ on 11½ pt.
15-0406-54230

Printed and bound in Great Britain
by Antony Rowe Ltd, Chippenham, Wiltshire

CHAPTER ONE

WELCOME TO CROCODILE CREEK!

The writing was gold on green, very patriotic, but what was a woman who'd grown up in a penthouse in inner city Melbourne, and to whom wildlife was a friend's pet galah, doing in a place called Crocodile Creek?

She'd overreacted.

Again!

Though flinging her engagement ring at Lindy hadn't really been overreacting—it had been a necessary release of tension to avoid killing either her erstwhile best friend or her stunned and now ex-fiancé, Daniel.

Overwhelmed by the sign telling her she'd finally reached her destination, Kate pulled the car over onto the grass verge and stared at the name of the town, heart thudding erratically at the magnitude of what she'd done, and with apprehension of what might lie ahead.

Could this unlikely place with the corny name—Crocodile Creek, as if!—possibly provide the answers she so desperately needed to rebuild her life?

She then considered the implications of the town's name again. Nah! Surely nobody would build a town on a creek that actually had crocodiles in it.

But she glanced behind her towards what looked like, well,

more like a river than a creek—and, just in case, put the car into gear again and drove on.

Up here in North Queensland anything might be possible.

'Go through the town, over the bridge, past the hospital to a big house on a bluff.'

The directions the director of nursing had given on the phone last night had been clear enough. The road led through the town and over another rather rickety bridge. Looking out her side window, Kate was tempted to stop again, for there, virtually in the middle of the town, was a sandy beach, lapped by lazy waves that frilled the edge of a blue-green sea. Hot and sticky from this final day of a five-day drive, she looked with longing at the water, but someone called Hamish was expecting her at the house.

The house!

Could that be it?

The one perched on the bluff at the southern end of this magical cove?

As a child she'd dreamed of living in a house by the sea, a longing frustrated rather than satisfied by holidays at the beach.

Excited now, she drove on. Yes, that was definitely a hospital on her right. Low set and relatively modern, it was surrounded by palms and bright-leafed plants, but still had the usual signs to Emergency, Admittance and parking areas.

Past the hospital she went, to the house on the hill—by the sea—parked the car in a small paved area to one side, unloaded her suitcase and climbed the steps to the wide veranda.

The front door was open, but she tapped on it anyway, then called out a tentative hello before venturing slowly down the wide hall that seemed to lead right through the middle of the old building.

'Have you any idea how difficult it is to organise a rodeo?'

The big man appeared at the far end of the hall, waving the

handset of the phone as he spoke. A soft Scottish accent spun the question from bizarre to fantasy and when he added, 'You'll be Kate, then?' in that intriguing voice, Kate smiled for the first time in about six months.

Well, maybe not quite six months.

'I will be, then,' she said, dropping her suitcase and coming towards him with her hand held out. 'Kate Winship. When I phoned last night the DON said Hamish would show me around the house, so you'll be Hamish?'

His large firm hand engulfed hers and the voice said, 'Hamish McGregor,' but something apart from the accent made Kate look up—into eyes so dark a blue they looked almost black, here in the shadowy hall of the big old house she'd been told was called 'the doctors' house'.

She removed her hand from his and backed away. One step. Two. Then she realised she must look stupid and backed far enough to turn her panicky retreat into a suitcase retrieval.

'I'll take that.'

He only needed one long stride, lifting it from her unresisting fingers.

'We've put you in here. This was Mike's room, but he and— Well, you'll get to know everyone soon enough. Suffice it to say there're more people sharing rooms these days than there used to be, which is why we've room for some of the nursing staff while the nurses' quarters are renovated.'

He turned a teasing smile on Kate.

'Fair warning, Nurse Winship. There's been an epidemic of love racing through Crocodile Creek these past few weeks, so watch how you go.'

'Love! That's the last thing I'll catch,' she assured him. 'I'm immunised, inoculated *and* vaccinated. The love bug won't bite *me*.'

He set her suitcase on the bed and turned to look at her, dark eyebrows rising to meet brown-black hair that flopped in a heavy clump over his forehead. The eyebrows were asking questions, friendly questions, but there was no way she was going to answer them. The hurting was too new—too confusing—too all-encompassing. She had to learn to cope with it herself before she could share it with anyone—*if* she could ever share it.

But he was still watching her.

Waiting…

Diversion time.

'Why are you organising a rodeo?'

His smile returned, softening his rather austere features, parting lips to reveal strong white teeth.

All the better to eat you with, Kate reminded herself as a niggle of something she didn't want to feel stirred inside her.

'It's for the swimming pool.'

'Of course—a swimming pool for bulls and bucking horses.'

A deep, rich chuckle accompanied the smile this time. Had she not been immune…

'We're raising funds for a swimming pool at Wygera, an aboriginal community about fifty miles inland. The kids are bored to death—literally to death in some cases—sniffing petrol, chroming, drag racing, killing themselves for excitement.'

The smile had faded and his now sombre tone told her he'd experienced the anger and frustration medical staff inevitably felt at the senseless loss of young lives.

'And when's this rodeo?'

'Weekend after next. That's why the house is deserted. Whoever's off duty is out at Wygera, organising things there—not so much for the rodeo as for the competition for a design for the swimming pool. Entries have to be in by today and the staff available are out there registering them and sorting them into categories. All the locals are involved. I'm on call for the emergency service. Did you know we have both a plane and a helicopter based—?'

The phone interrupted his explanation, and as he walked out of the room to speak to the caller, Kate opened her suitcase and stared at the contents neatly packed inside. But her mind wasn't seeing T-shirts and underwear, it was seeing young indigenous Australians, so bored they killed themselves with paint or petrol fumes.

You're here to trace your mother's life, not save the world. But the image remained until Hamish materialised in the doorway.

'Look,' he said, brushing the rebellious hair back from his forehead. 'I hate to ask this when you've just arrived, but would you mind doing an emergency flight with me? There are fifteen kids from a birthday party throwing up over at the hospital so the staff there have their hands full.'

Kate closed her suitcase.

'Take me to your aircraft,' she said.

'When you've put something sensible on your feet. Nice as purple flowery sandals might be, they won't give much protection to your ankles if we have to be lowered to the patient.'

'Are you criticising my footwear?' she said lightly, embarrassed that he'd even noticed what she was wearing on her feet. Embarrassed by the frivolous flowers.

She opened her case again and dug into the bottom of it to find her sensible walking boots. The rest of her outfit was eminently practical. Chocolate brown calf-length pants, and a paler brown T-shirt with just one purple flower decorating the shoulder. But a woman couldn't be sensible right down to her toes—especially not when these delicious sandals had called to her from a shop window in Townsville the day before.

Pulling off the sandals, she sat down on the bed to put on her boots, uncomfortably aware that Hamish hadn't answered her.

Uncomfortably aware of Hamish.

'You don't have to wait—just tell me where to go. Is it to the airport? I passed that on the way in.'

'Regular clinic flights leave from the airport. And retrievals leave from there if the aircraft is being used. But today it's the chopper.'

He didn't move from the doorway and Kate was pleased when she finally had her boots laced tightly and was ready to leave.

She followed him through the house, out the back door and into a beautiful, scented garden. She glanced around, trying to identify the source of the perfume that lingered in the air, but Hamish was striding on, unaffected by the beauty. Too used to it, she guessed.

'We've a helipad behind the hospital to save double transferring of patients,' Hamish explained. 'The service has two helicopter pilots and one of them, Mike Poulos, is also a paramedic, so we can do rescue flights with just him and a doctor, but when he's off duty and Rex is flying, we take two medical staff.'

'Is it a traffic accident?' Kate was glad she'd been running every morning. Keeping up with Hamish's long strides meant she had to trot along beside him.

'Apparently not.'

It was such a strange response she glanced towards the man who'd made it and saw him frowning at his thoughts.

'It was a weird call and, now I think about it, maybe you shouldn't come,' he added.

'I'm coming. Weird what way? Domestic situation?'

'No, just weird. The caller said there was an injured man in Cabbage Palm Gorge and gave a GPS reading. You know about satellite global positioning systems?'

'I've heard of it but, generally speaking, street names are more useful in Melbourne. Corner of Collins and Swanson kind of thing.'

A glimmer of a smile chased the worry from his face, but not for long.

'Because it's a gorge, we might have to be lowered from the chopper.'

'Been there and done that, though not, admittedly, into a gorge. But I have been lowered onto an oil-rig in Bass Strait in a gale, and that's not a lot of fun, believe me.'

They'd reached the helicopter, and the conversation stopped while Hamish introduced Rex, a middle-aged man with a bald head and luxuriant moustache, then they clambered into the overalls he handed them.

'It's three-quarters of an hour to the head of the gorge, but until we're over it and get the right GPS reading, we won't know where the bloke is. I can't land anywhere in the gorge itself, and going down on the winch without a landing spot marked isn't an option in that country—too thickly treed. So I'll land where I can at the top of the gorge and you'll have to abseil down.'

Rex was talking to Hamish, but glancing warily at Kate from time to time.

'That's fine,' she assured him before Hamish could answer. 'I'm qualified for that and did a winch-refresher weekend only a month or so ago.'

Taken because she'd thought she'd be going back to the emergency department at St Stephen's and on roster for rescue missions...

'We'll see,' Hamish objected. 'I think I should go down first to find the patient. If he's mobile, we won't need two people.'

'No go, Doc!' Rex told him, hustling them into the cabin, handing Kate some headphones then checking she'd found her seat belt. 'It'll be dusk by the time we get there and, though it's not as deep as Carnarvon or Cobbold Gorge, Cabbage Palm's no picnic. Even if you find a suitable place to lift him from, I won't be able to do it tonight. And RRS rules say two staff for overnighters.'

RRS—Remote Rescue Service, Kate worked out. She hadn't realised when she'd asked the agency for a job at

Crocodile Creek that it had such wide-ranging services. She glanced at the man with whom she was about to spend the night. He was frowning again.

'Do you suffer some kind of knight errantry towards women, that you're looking so grim?'

Because he wasn't yet wearing his headphones, she had to yell the question above the noise of the engines. He turned towards her and shrugged, but didn't reply. Which was fine by her. Helicopters weren't the best places for casual conversation.

They lifted off the ground and Kate wriggled around so she could see out the window. The hospital was cradled by the curve of a creek—no doubt called Crocodile—to the west, but to the east there must be a view of the blue waters of the cove. She could see the doctors house on the bluff overlooking the cove, then the stretch of sand and water and another bluff on the northern end, on which perched a sprawling, white-painted building set in lush tropical gardens.

Beyond the creek, on the landward side, was a reasonably sized town, a cluster of larger buildings lining the main road. She'd driven past them earlier, noticing a pub, a grocery store and a hairdressing salon.

The helicopter swung away, and now all Kate could see were the slopes of hills, many of them covered with banana planta-tions, while beyond them rainforest-clad mountains rose up to meet the sky.

'It's cattle country once we're over the mountains.'

She turned to Hamish and nodded acceptance of his state-ment, soon seeing for herself the open stretches of tree-studded plains. Rex seemed to be following what appeared to be a river, with more closely packed trees marking its meandering course. Then more hills appeared, rugged, rocky sentinels rising sheer from the plains, the setting sun catching their cliffs and turning them ruby red and scarlet.

So this was what people talked about when they used

phrases like 'red centre' to describe Australia. Kate pressed her face to the window to get a better view.

'You'll be seeing it firsthand before long,' Hamish reminded her, and, right on cue, the helicopter began to descend. It took another twenty minutes but eventually Rex found somewhere he could safely set down. He turned off the engine and, with the rotor blades slowing, he climbed back into the cabin and began to unstrap the equipment they would need.

'I'll send you down first, Doc, then the gear, then you, Sister Winship.'

'Kate, please,' Kate protested, but Rex just shook his head.

'Rex is an old-fashioned gentleman. He calls all the women by their proper titles,' Hamish told her. 'Tried to call me Dr McGregor for the first few months I was here, but I kept thinking he must be talking to my father and didn't answer, so he finally gave it up.'

Hamish was checking the equipment bags as he spoke. Once satisfied that each contained what it should, he'd lower it out of the helicopter. Rex set up a belay rope, using one of the helicopter's skids as the anchor point, and Kate was reassured by the professionalism of both men.

'You've got the radio but once I leave the top of the gorge you won't be able to contact me until I'm back overhead in the morning. Use the hand-held GPS to find the patient. When it's light, if you can see a space—maybe near the waterhole— that's clear enough for me to do a stretcher lift, you can radio me the position.' Rex was looking anxiously at Hamish, obviously unhappy that he had to abandon the two of them. 'I'll fly over to Wetherby Downs for the night, refuel and be in the air again at first light. Back here soon after six.'

'We'll be OK,' Hamish assured him, handing an abseiling harness to Kate, then fastening himself into a similar one. He followed this up with a helmet, complete with headlamp. 'Kate, you're sure you're happy about this? You could stay with Rex.

It wouldn't be the first time we've broken RRS rules in an emergency.'

'Not on my first day,' Kate joked, hiding a tremor of trepidation. The gorge wasn't all that deep, and dropping down the cliff-face would be simple, but the sun had already left the bottom of the cleft and the shadowy gloom beneath them seemed…unwelcoming somehow.

She watched Hamish disappear, and when he gave the signal helped Rex haul the reinforced rope back up. They hooked the two backpacks, one with medical gear and the other with the stretcher and stabilising equipment, onto the rope, then added another which, Rex explained, held emergency rations.

'There's a little gas stove so you'll be able to have a hot cuppa later tonight,' he said. 'No fires, though, it's a national park.'

Kate nodded, though she was certain park rangers would forgive a small fire should it be needed for warmth or survival.

She watched as Rex lowered the rope. Hamish would undo the gear, then send the rope back up, and it would be her turn.

Strong arms caught and steadied her as she found her feet, then Hamish unclipped her harness and signalled to Rex he could haul it back up. But the pilot was obviously anxious for he repeated all his warnings and instructions about contact before Hamish finally signed off.

He reached down and swung one of the backpacks onto his shoulders, then lifted the other one.

'That's mine,' Kate told him. 'If you want to be gallant, take the smaller bag.'

He grumbled to himself, but held the medical equipment pack up for her so she could slip her arms into the straps.

'We've a way to walk,' he warned, and Kate grinned at him.

'My legs may not be as long as yours, but they'll get me anywhere we need to go, so lead on.'

He muttered something that sounded like 'damned independent women,' then turned his attention to the GPS, marking their current position as Landmark One, then keying in the position of the injured man.

'It's about eight hundred yards in that direction,' he said, showing Kate the route map that had come up on the small screen.

They set off, picking their way through the wide-leafed palms that gave the gorge its name, clambering over the rocks littering the banks of the narrow creek that had cut through the sandstone over millions of years to form the deep but narrow valley. The creek was dry now, at the end of winter, but, come the wet season in late October, and it would roar to life, marks on the cliffs showing how high it could rise.

Darkness was falling swiftly, but they'd left the creek-bank and were walking on more stable ground, the light from their torches picking out any traps for their feet.

'It shouldn't be far now,' Hamish told her. 'I'll try a "coo-ee."'

The thought of a Scot using the Australian bush call made Kate smile, but Hamish's 'coo-ee' was loud and strong, echoing back to them off the cliffs. Then they heard it, faint but clear, definitely a reply.

'Well, at least he's conscious,' Hamish said, reaching back to take Kate's hand to guide her in the right direction—hurrying now they knew they were close to their patient.

The man was lying propped against the base of the cliffs, an overhang above him forming a shallow, open cave. A very young man, haggard with pain, trying hard to hold back tears he no doubt felt were unmanly.

'Digger said he'd let someone know, but I thought he was just saying it to make himself feel better about leaving me,' the lad whispered, his voice choking and breaking on the words.

'Well, he did the job and here we are,' Hamish told him. 'One doctor and one nurse, all present and correct. I'm Hamish and this is Kate, who'd barely set foot in Crocodile Creek when we whisked her off on this adventure.'

'Crocodile Creek? You're from Crocodile Creek?'

He sounded panicky and Kate knelt beside him and took his hand, feeling heat beneath his dry skin.

'We're the Remote Rescue Service,' she said gently. 'And now you know us, who are you and what have you done to yourself?'

She brushed her free hand against his cheek, confirming her first impression of a fever, then rested it on his chest, unobtrusively counting his respiratory rate. Twenty-five. Far too fast. She'd get him onto oxygen while Hamish completed his assessment.

The Scottish doctor was already kneeling on the other side of their patient, taking his pulse with one hand while the other released the clasps on the backpack. Kate swung hers to the ground and moved so her light swept over the patient's body, picking up a rough, blood-stained bandage around the young man's right thigh.

'There's a bullet in my leg,' he said, and the phrasing of the answer made Hamish frown, although he didn't question how or why, simply repeating part of Kate's question.

'And your name?'

The lad hesitated for another few seconds then finally said, 'Jack. My name's Jack.'

He was radiating tension that Kate guessed was more to do with his circumstances than his condition, although he seemed very weak. But if his tension arose from being abandoned, injured, in the middle of nowhere, surely their arrival should have brought relief.

And the name? Had he opted for Jack as a common enough name or was he really a Jack? Kate didn't know, but she did know it didn't matter. Jack he would be while they tended him, and part of tending him would be getting him to relax.

Hamish was doing his best, chatting as he ran his hands over Jack's head and neck, asking him questions all the time, satisfying himself there were no other wounds and no reason to suspect internal damage. Where was the pain? Could he feel this? This? Had he come off his horse? Off a bike? Hit his head at all?

Jack's responses were guarded, and occasionally confused, but, no, he hadn't fallen, he'd stayed right on his bike. It was a four-wheeler.

And where was the bike?

He looked vaguely around, then shook his head, as if uncertain where a four-wheeler bike might have disappeared to.

The smell hit Kate as she fitted a mask and tube to the small oxygen bottle she'd taken from her backpack. She looked up to see Hamish unwinding the bandage from Jack's leg. Necrotic tissue—no wonder the boy was feverish and looked so haggard.

'How long since it happened?'

Jack shrugged.

'Yesterday, I think. Or maybe the day before. I've been feeling pretty sick—went to sleep. Didn't wake up until Digger moved me here this morning.'

'Where's Digger now?' Kate asked, holding the oxygen mask away from his face so he could answer.

'Dunno.'

Hamish raised his eyebrows at Kate, but didn't comment, saying instead, 'His pulse is racing. He needs fluid fast. I don't want to do a cut-down here, so we'll run it into both arms. If you open the smaller pack you'll find a lamp. Set it up first then in your pack there'll be all we need for fluid resuscitation— 16g cannulae and infusers for rapid delivery. You'll see the crystalloid solutions clearly marked.'

Kate found the battery-operated lamp and turned it on, a bright fluorescent light pushing back the shadowy evening.

Now it was easy to see what they had—sterile packs of cannulas and catheters, bags of fluid, battery-operated fluid warmers, boxes of drugs.

'Good luck,' she said to Hamish as she handed him a venipuncture kit. 'We're going to get some fluid flowing into you,' she added to Jack, as she found the fluid Hamish wanted and began to warm the first bag. 'And that means inserting a hollow needle into one of your veins. But because you're pretty dehydrated, your veins will have gone flat so it won't be an easy job. I'm betting Hamish will need at least two goes to get it in.'

'I'll have you know, Sister Winship, I'm known as One-Go McGregor,' Hamish said huffily, taking the tourniquet Kate passed him and winding it around Jack's upper arm, hoping to raise a vein in the back of his hand or his wrist.

The needle slipped in. 'See, told you!' Hamish turned triumphantly to Jack. 'Aren't you glad you didn't bet?'

Kate had tubing and a bag of fluid ready, and she turned her light onto the cliff-face behind their patient in search of small ledges where they could place the bags.

They changed places, Kate starting the fluid flowing into Jack's vein, then setting the bag so it would continue to gravity feed through the tube. And all the time she talked to him—not about how he'd come to have a bullet in his leg, but about what she was doing, and how it would help.

'Once Hamish has you hooked up on that side, we can start pain relief and antibiotics. It's the infection from your wound that's making you feel so lousy.'

'Actually,' Hamish said mildly, 'getting shot in the first place would make me feel pretty lousy.'

Jack gave a snort of laughter, and relief flowed through Kate. Surely if he could laugh he'd be OK. But he was very weak and the wound, now she could see it, was a mess. A deeply scored indentation running from halfway down his thigh towards his hip, then disappearing into a puckered, blue-rimmed hole. Dried blood on the bandages suggested it had bled freely—but not freely enough to keep infection at bay.

Hamish set the second bag of fluid on the ledge behind Jack, then probed through the contents of the backpack.

'I'll get some antibiotics into you with that fluid, then I want to check your distal pulses and test sensation in your foot and lower leg. Kate, would you watch for renewed bleeding from the wound? We know you've been lucky, Jack, in that the bullet didn't go into your femoral artery. And how do we know that?'

Hamish had found what he wanted—a small bag of fluid Kate recognised as IV antibiotic medication diluted with saline. He spiked it with an IV administration set, connected it to a second port in the IV line he had running, then placed the small bag on the ledge so the drug could be administered simultaneously with the fluid.

'Because you'd have bled to death by now—that's how we know the bullet didn't hit your artery,' he said cheerfully. 'But it might have damaged a nerve, which is why I'm going to prick your foot, or the velocity of the bullet might have chipped a bone and sent that as a secondary missile to squeeze against the artery, which is why I'm going to check to see if blood is still flowing in your foot.'

Kate watched Jack's face and saw that Hamish's matter-of-fact approach was just what the young man needed. In fact, he was interested enough to ask, 'Why does Kate have to watch for bleeding?'

'Good question! Go to the top of the class.' Hamish smiled at him. 'Kate has to watch because you'll have damaged some blood vessels, but smaller veins and capillaries have the ability to close themselves off if that happens. Problem is, once we build up your fluid levels, they might get all excited and open up again—bleeding all over the place.'

'Ouch!'

Jack jerked his leg, and the bleeding Kate was watching for began right on cue.

'Well, you've feeling in your toes and a weak but palpable pulse in your ankle, so I'd say you've been a very lucky young man. Unfortunately, that luck's about to change. I need to clean up that wound and, although I'll anaesthetise the area around it with a local, it won't be comfortable. Kate, how about you shift over to Jack's other side and talk to him while I work? Can you talk and pass instruments and dressings?'

Kate stared at the man who was taking this situation so calmly, chatting away to Jack as if they were sharing space on a city bus, not a cave at the bottom of a gorge at nightfall, while someone with a gun lurked somewhere in the darkness.

'Well?'

Hamish smiled at her and she shook her head, then realised he might think she was answering his question.

'Of course I can talk and pass things,' she said, immediately regretting the assurance when his smile broadened and he threw a conspiratorial wink at Jack.

'I thought so,' he gloated. 'Most women can talk and do other things, can't they, mate?'

Jack smiled back while Kate glowered at the pair of them. She'd walked right into that one.

'Local anaesthesia is in the green box,' Hamish continued, 'and sterile swabs in the white one with the red writing. You might pass me the sharps container and a plastic bag out of that pack as well, so I can put the soiled stuff away as I use it.'

Kate handed him what he needed, then checked the contents of the pack again, trying to anticipate what Hamish would want next. A scalpel, no doubt, to cut away some of the infected tissue, and more swabs to mop up blood as he got down to clean flesh.

Sutures? Would he stitch it up or leave it open until they got back to the hospital where further surgery would be necessary?

She set out what she thought he'd need immediately, placed

them on a large flat stone and lifted it across Jack so it was within Hamish's reach.

'You're supposed to be talking to me,' Jack reminded her, but his voice was weaker than it had been earlier. Seeing them had probably prompted a surge in his adrenaline levels which had now waned. Did Hamish want her talking to the young man to distract him, or to keep him awake and stop him slipping into unconsciousness?

Not that the reason mattered.

'I will,' she promised, checking his blood pressure, pulse and respirations. He had the mask across his mouth and nose, but was talking easily through it. His breathing was still far too fast, but his pulse, though still tachycardic, was more regular than it had been when she'd automatically felt it earlier. 'You start. Tell me all about yourself.'

'Not worth talking about,' he muttered weakly. 'In fact, I'd have been better off if you hadn't come.'

'And here I thought you were pleased to see us,' Kate teased, aware a little self-pity was quite normal in someone so ill.

'Well, I was at first,' Jack grudgingly admitted, 'but only because I was feeling so lousy. Really, though, I'd be better off dead.'

'Don't we all feel that at times?' Kate sighed.

'I bet you don't,' Jack retorted, buying into the argument she'd provoked, although he was so weak. 'Look at you—pretty, probably well dressed under those overalls, good job. What would someone like you know about how I feel?'

'I would if you told me.' Kate smiled at him. 'In fact, you tell me the Jack story and I'll tell you the Kate story, and I bet I can beat your misery with my misery—hands down.'

'I bet you can't.'

'I bet I can.'

'Bet you can't!'

'Can!'

'Children, just get on with it.'

Hamish's voice was pained, but Kate heard amusement in it as well. He knew they had to find out Jack's background, and had guessed this was her way of goading Jack into telling it.

'My family didn't want me,' Jack began, anxiety and pain tightening the words so they caused a sympathetic lurch of pain in Kate's chest. 'They all live in Sydney and they sent me right up here to work. Can you imagine a family doing that?'

'Not to a nice boy like you,' Kate told him, taking his hand to offer comfort even while she tried to stir him into further revelations. 'But mine's worse. My father died, then my mother, then my brother told me they weren't my parents at all. They'd just brought me up because they'd felt sorry for me. So I didn't really have a family at all. Beat that.'

Jack frowned at her, but had his comeback ready.

'Mine'll disinherit me when they find out about this,' he said.

'Well, that sounds as if they haven't already done it. You've still got time to redeem yourself. And now you're hurt, you can play the sympathy card. My brother—or the louse I thought was my brother—is contesting my mother's will because he says I wasn't ever properly adopted. How's that for the ultimate disinheritance?'

'That *is* a lousy thing to do,' Jack agreed, but he was thinking hard, obviously not yet ready to concede in the misery stakes. 'My uncle kicked me off his property.'

'I traced my birth mother but found out she'd died the week before I got there.'

'Wow! That's terrible. So you don't know who you are?'

'Nobody—that's who I am,' Kate said cheerfully. She didn't feel cheerful about it, but that wasn't the point. Keeping Jack talking was the point. 'Beat you, didn't I?'

He looked at her for a moment then shook his head.

'I lost my girl.'

His voice broke on the words and Kate squeezed harder on his hand.

'That's why my uncle kicked me out.'

'Ah, that's terrible, but can't you get in touch with her again even if you're not working for your uncle?'

Jack shook his head.

'I tried. I really tried. I worked on another property. It didn't pay much so I got this other job, then I had some time off so I thought I'd go and see her—tell her what was happening. But I couldn't get a lift—I tried, I really tried—and I had to get back, and it turned out— Anyway, if I had got to her place, her dad would probably have killed me. It was her dad broke us up. He rang my uncle and told him we'd been seeing each other. Apparently he went mental about it and that's why my uncle sacked me.'

The story had come tumbling out in confused snatches, but Kate was able to piece it all together.

'Love problems are the pits,' she sympathised, 'but, really, yours are chicken feed, Jack.'

'Chicken feed?' He perked up at the challenge she offered him. 'I'm shot and I lost my girl.'

'OK, but what about this? I stop work to nurse my mother—'

'Who wasn't your mother,' Jack offered.

'That's right, but I loved her.' It was only with difficulty Kate stopped her own voice cracking. This wasn't personal, it was professional, and Jack was sounding much more alert. 'Anyway, I took two months off to nurse her at the end and my ever-loving fiancé and my best friend began an affair right under the noses of all our colleagues. OK, so I didn't lose my job, but can you imagine going back to work with the pair of them billing and cooing all over the place, and everyone laughing about it?'

'More swabs.'

The gruff demand reminded Kate that Jack wasn't the only one hearing the story of her recent life, but Hamish had told her to distract Jack, and her strategy was working. She opened a new packet of swabs and passed them over, giving Hamish a look that warned him not to say one thing about her conversation.

'No, I wouldn't have gone back to work there either,' Jack said. 'But you've got another job now, haven't you? I'll never get another job.'

'Piffle! Of course you will. Young, healthy, good-looking chap like you. You'll get another job and another girl, both better than the ones before.'

Silence greeted this remark, a silence that stretched for so long Kate checked his pulse again. Then he said quietly, 'I don't want another girl, and I don't know how to get…the one I want back now I've messed things up so much.'

'We'll help you,' Kate promised rashly. 'Won't we, Hamish? We'll get you better then we'll help you find your girl.'

Hamish looked up from the business of debriding infected tissue from Jack's leg.

'We can certainly try,' he said, but the frown on his face was denying his words.

Did he think they wouldn't find the girl?

Or…Kate's heart paused a beat…did he think they wouldn't get this young man better?

CHAPTER TWO

'OKAY, THAT'S ABOUT as clean as I can get it without actually removing the bullet,' Hamish announced. 'I'd like to go in and get it, but without X-rays to show us exactly where it is and where I'd have to cut, I wouldn't risk it. You're also losing a fair bit of blood, Jack. Had any problems with bleeding before?'

Jack ignored the question, closing his eyes as if the effort of talking to Kate had exhausted him.

Which it might have, though Hamish was thinking otherwise.

'At least, doing it back at the hospital, we'll have blood on hand should you need it. The helicopter will be back at first light, and we'll have you in Theatre in Crocodile Creek a couple of hours later.'

Jack's eyes opened at that, and he tried to sit up straighter.

'Shouldn't I go to Cairns? Or what about Townsville? That has a bigger hospital, doesn't it?'

'Bigger but not better,' Hamish told him. 'Besides, it's too far for a chopper flight. Something about Crocodile Creek bothering you? We don't really have crocodiles in the creek— well, not where it flows past the hospital.'

Jack didn't answer, but turned his head away, as if not seeing Hamish might remove him from the cave.

And the prospect of a trip to Crocodile Creek…

Hamish watched Kate bend to speak quietly to the young man, no doubt reassuring him he'd have the very best of treatment at Crocodile Creek, but Hamish was becoming more and more certain that Jack had reasons of his own for avoiding that particular hospital.

But how to confirm what he was thinking?

He walked around to the other side and squatted beside the open pack, delving through it for what he needed. Then, from this side, he looked directly at Jack.

'I'll add some pain relief to the fluid now, so you should be feeling more comfortable before long, and then I guess we should do the paperwork. You up for that, Kate? Did you see the initial assessment forms in the pack?'

Kate's frown told him she disapproved of the change in his attitude from friendly banter to practical matter-of-factness, but she didn't know about a feud between two neighbouring families up here in the north, or the connection of one family to the hospital. Or about a baby called Lucky who was now called Jackson who had a form of haemophilia known as von Willebrand's disease.

Or about the search for the baby's father—a young man called Jack.

'I've got them here,' she said, putting ice into her words in case he hadn't caught the frown.

'Then fill them out. You and Jack can manage all the personal stuff then I'll do the medication and dosages when you get down to that section. And while you're doing it, I'll take a look around to see if there's a patch of clear ground from which we can winch Jack up in the morning.'

He found a stronger torch in the equipment backpack, turned it on and walked away, hoping his absence might help Jack speak more freely. If he'd talk to anyone, it would be to Kate. Nothing like a baring of souls to create a bond between people. But had she really been through so much emotional trauma or had she made it all up to keep Jack talking? He had no idea, which wasn't surprising, but what did surprise him was that he wanted to find out.

Hell's teeth! He'd been in Australia for nearly two years, and while he'd enjoyed some mild flirtations and one reasonably lengthy and decidedly pleasant relationship, he'd remained heart-whole and fancy-free. So now, three weeks before he was due to return home, was hardly the time to be developing an interest in a woman.

Yet his mind kept throwing up the image of his first sight of her, a slight figure, dressed all in brown, except for those ridiculous purple sandals, standing in the gloomy hallway, with a stray sunbeam probing through the fretwork breezeway above the door and turning the tips of her loose brown curls to liquid gold.

'Is he a good doctor?' Jack asked, when Hamish had disappeared into the darkness.

Kate looked in the direction Hamish had taken, but already she could see nothing but inky blackness beyond the glow of the lamp.

'I've just started work so I don't know, but from the way he treated you I'd have to say he is.'

Jack closed his eyes and lay in silence for a while, but just when Kate had decided he'd drifted off to sleep he opened his eyes again and looked at her.

'So you don't know anything about the hospital?' he asked.

'Not a thing, except its reputation is excellent. Apparently the boss, Charles Wetherby, insists on hiring top-class staff and only buying the best equipment, so it has a name for being far in advance of most country hospitals.'

But her words failed to reassure Jack, who had not only closed his eyes but had now folded his lips into a straight line of worry.

Seeking to divert him, she pulled out the pad of assessment forms.

'You must be tired, but before you drop off to sleep, how about we fill this out. There aren't many questions.'

Jack opened his eyes and looked directly at her.

'I should have died,' he said, then he closed his eyes again and turned his head away, making it unmistakably clear that the conversation was over.

'Full name?' Kate asked hopefully. 'Address? Come on, Jack, we have to do this.'

But the young man had removed himself from her—not physically, but mentally—cutting the link she'd thought she'd forged when they'd played their 'whose life sucks the most' game earlier.

She lifted his wrist and checked his pulse then wrote the time and the rate on the form. She filled in all the other parts she could, remembering Jack's initial respiration rate, systolic blood pressure—she'd taken that herself before Hamish had started the second drip—and pulse, writing times and numbers, wondering about all the unanswered questions at the top of the form.

'Asleep?'

Hamish's quiet question preceded him into the light. She stood up, careful not to disturb their patient, and moved a little away.

'He wasn't—just closed his eyes to avoid answering me—but I think he's genuinely asleep now. I've just checked him. His pulse is steadier but his systolic blood pressure hasn't changed as much as I'd have thought it would, considering the fluid we're giving him. Do you think there could be internal bleeding somewhere?'

'It's likely, and though I've sutured part of the wound and put a pressure pad on it, I'd say it's still bleeding.'

'That's more than a guess, isn't it?' Kate looked up at the man who sounded so concerned. They'd moved out of the lamplight, but a full moon had risen and was shedding soft, silvery light into the gorge.

'It's a long story but we've time ahead of us. If you dig into the equipment backpack you'll find a space blanket to wrap around Jack—there should be a couple of inflatable pillows in there as well. Put one under his feet and one behind his head and cover him with the blanket while I get a cuppa going and find something for us to eat.'

'And then you'll tell me?'

Hamish smiled, but it was a grim effort.

'I'll tell you what I'm guessing.'

Kate cupped her hands around the now empty mug and looked out at the broad leaves of the cabbage palms that filled the gorge. Hamish's story of a newborn baby found at a rodeo, the dramatic efforts that had saved his life, the finding of his dangerously ill mother, and the fight to save *her* life, was the stuff of television medicine, while feuding neighbours and heart attacks turned it into soap opera.

Maybe she'd got it wrong.

She turned to Hamish, sitting solidly beside her at the entrance to the cave.

'So you think Jack is Charles Wetherby's nephew, sacked from the family property, run by Charles's brother Philip, for consorting with the Cooper girl, daughter of the Wetherbys' sworn enemies who live next door. And you've put all this together because his wound is bleeding and you think he has von Willebrand's disease.'

'Lucky—the baby—has von Willebrand's disease and it runs through the Wetherby family,' Hamish said patiently. 'Originally, back when Lucky was found, Charles had no idea his nephew had been working at Wetherby Downs, because Charles and Philip rarely spoke to each other. But since Jim Cooper was admitted to hospital with a heart attack, Charles has been anxious about the Coopers' property and that forced him to speak to Philip—'

'Who told him about Jack and Megan—OK, I get that bit,'

Kate assured him. 'And the family feud—I can understand that. But if Jack is Charles's nephew, and Charles and Philip don't get on, why's Jack so against going to hospital at Crocodile Creek? It's a good uncle and bad uncle scenario—like good cop and bad cop. You'd think he'd be happy to be under his good uncle's care. Family does count, you know.'

Before the words were fully out, she knew they were a mistake. She didn't need to look at Hamish to know those darned expressive eyebrows of his would be on the rise.

'Look,' she told him, wishing she was standing up and a little further away from him but resigned to making the best of things. 'The story I told Jack—well, that comes under the heading of nurse-patient confidentiality so, please, pretend you never heard it and don't you dare breathe so much as a word of it to anyone. I went back to work for a week after my mother died, and if one more person had put their arm around me or thrown me a "poor Kate" look, I tell you, I'd have slit their throat with the nearest scalpel. Stuff happens, and you have to move on. I've moved on, and that's it.'

He nodded but didn't speak. In the end she had to prompt him.

'So why's Jack worried about going to Crocodile Creek?'

'He has a bullet in his leg.'

Kate turned to frown at the man beside her.

'This is the bush. Out here, from what I've heard, people tote guns all the time. They shoot things—wild pigs and water buffalo and snakes. From the evidence of road signs on the drive up, they even shoot road signs. So he shot himself, gun going off as he climbed through a fence—isn't that what happens? Or maybe Digger shot him by accident.'

'So where's Digger now? If he shot Jack by accident, why would he call for help then disappear?'

'Because he had to be elsewhere. Had to take his cattle to market or organise a rodeo. I'm a city girl, how would I know where he had to be?'

She saw the glimmer of white teeth as Hamish smiled, but the cheerful expression passed quickly.

'Outback people aren't like that. They don't desert their mates. And Jack's worried about being disinherited for something that's happened since his uncle sacked him. My guess is he met up with some unsavoury characters—no doubt innocently, he's a city kid too, remember—and when he realised something was wrong, he tried to leave.'

'And someone shot him? To stop him leaving? Someone who's out there? With a gun?'

Kate must have sounded more panicky than she'd realised, for Hamish put a comforting arm around her shoulders and drew her close. It was probably a 'poor Kate' kind of hug and she should have been reaching for a scalpel, but the heavy arm was exceedingly comforting so she let it stay there—even snuggled a little closer.

Not a good idea as far as the immunity was concerned. She unsnuggled and thought a little more about Hamish's hypothesis.

'What kind of unsavoury characters might you have out here?'

'Cattle duffers.'

'Stupid cattle?'

Hamish laughed.

'Cattle thieves. They steal cattle from properties in the area. These properties are the size of small countries so their boundaries can't be watched all the time. The duffers keep the cattle somewhere safe—this gorge would be ideal—until they can alter the brands, then truck them to the markets.'

'So Jack meets these guys who say come and steal some cattle with us and he does?' She turned to study their sleeping patient for a moment. 'He doesn't look that dumb.'

Hamish turned to look as well, bringing his body closer.

'No, but say he meets a couple of guys at a pub, and their story is that they're droving a mob of cattle to a railhead. Something like that. Jack joins, thinking they're OK, then

slowly works out there's something wrong. I'd say he recognised his uncle's brand on some of the cattle. He tries to leave
and the boss, who's about to reap a good reward for his thievery,
tries to stop him.'

'With a bullet?'

Bother the immunity. Kate scooted back to snuggle position
by Hamish's side.

'They play for keeps.' He tucked his arm back around her
as if it was the most natural thing in the world. 'It's my guess
he didn't shoot to kill the kid. In his mind, that gave Jack a
chance of survival and himself time to get the cattle away from
here. Jack was lucky the second guy, Digger, had a conscience.'

'That does explain Jack's concern, but surely if he went into
the job innocently, he can't be charged with cattle… What was
the word you used?'

'Duffing.'

Kate nodded. 'I like it. Cattle duffing. It has a ring to it,
doesn't it? Not quite as nasty as stealing.'

'Apparently it's gone on ever since Australia was first settled,
but that doesn't make it right, or legal. No, our Jack will be in
trouble. For a start, we have to report bullet wounds to the
police.'

'But if he's the father of the baby, and we know he loves the
girl because he told us so, then it's not very lucky for Lucky if
his father's in jail. We'll have to get him off the charge. Don't
people get a second chance? Or if he's responsible for the
police catching the duffers, won't he be rewarded, not
punished? Perhaps we could help catch the duffers?'

'Well, that gives me hope,' Hamish said.

Kate shifted reluctantly away from him so she could turn
and look into his face.

'Hope for what? What kind of hope?'

He grinned at her.

'Well, I thought earlier you'd only come closer to me

because you were worried about a gunman lurking out there somewhere, but if you're brave enough to take on a couple of armed desperados, then I guess you were cuddling up to me because you like me.'

He touched her lightly on the head, lifting one of her curls and twirling it around his finger.

Dangerous territory, finger twirls in hair that felt very... comforting?

Kate took a deep breath, sorted her thoughts into order, shifted out of hair-twirling distance and tried to explain.

'I do like you, what little I know of you, but I meant what I said about immunity, Hamish. Coming to Crocodile Creek is the first stage in getting on with my life. My birth mother came from here and I want to find out more about her—and who my father was. At the moment, I'm lost. Everything I believed in—the very foundations of my life, even love—proved to be a lie and right now I need to find some truths. Something to rebuild on. Can you understand that?'

He nodded, then stared out into the gorge for a few minutes before saying, 'I could help you, Kate. Everyone at the hospital would help you. Some of the staff have lived in Crocodile Creek all their lives.'

'No!'

The word came out far more strongly—and more loudly—than she'd intended, and she turned automatically to see if she'd disturbed Jack. He was still sleeping peacefully, so she repeated the word more quietly this time.

'No, Hamish. I know you mean well, but this is something I have to do myself.'

She'd edged further away from him and Hamish knew she was withdrawing behind whatever feeble defences she'd been able to build up since her callous brother and unfaithful rat of a fiancé had delivered their separate but equally devastating blows. He could understand her reluctance to accept help because accepting help meant getting close to the helper, and right now, with everything she'd ever trusted in stripped away from her, getting close to someone wasn't an option.

'OK,' he conceded. 'But just remember, if ever you need anything at all, a little help, a hug—especially a hug—I'll be there for you.'

'Thanks,' she said, but Hamish knew there was no way she'd be coming to him for a hug. She'd felt the same chemistry he had between them and hugs plus chemistry equalled trouble for a woman who claimed to be immune to love and who was fresh out of trust.

'I'll check our patient, then we should try to get some sleep,' he said, standing up and moving back into the cave. 'There are a couple more of those space blankets in the pack. It could get cold towards morning.'

Grateful to have something to do, Kate also stood. She'd noticed a couple more packs of the flimsy silver sheets they called space blankets when she'd pulled one out to cover Jack. She was aware they prevented heat loss from the body but was dubious about how warm they'd be if the night grew cold. Still, it was something to do and having something to do was important because it stopped her thinking about the mess her life was in. She'd talked bravely to Hamish of having to do this on her own, but it was the aloneness of her situation—the total stripping away of all she'd believed to be true—that frightened her the most. Far more than a man with a gun somewhere out there in the darkness of the gorge.

Hamish was attaching a new bag of fluid to one of Jack's IV lines. He nodded towards the blood-stained bandage.

'I'm just hoping it's not running out faster than it runs in.'

'Should we give him a clotting agent of some kind—or don't the packs carry such things?'

'They contain Thrombostat, which is topical thrombin. I put some on when I was dressing the wound. Because of Lucky, everyone at the hospital knows a lot more about von Willebrand's disease than most non-specialist physicians would but I don't know as much as I'd like to know. I know some coagulants work for some haemophilic patients and not others, depending on the missing blood factor in their particular disease. I wouldn't like to try anything on him without checking a pharmacology text for contraindications or complications…'

He paused and sighed, but Kate understood his dilemma.

'You don't want to take the risk,' she finished for him. 'Well, hopefully the thrombin will work well enough to stop some of the bleeding.'

'Externally!' Hamish reminded her, hanging the second fresh bag of fluid. 'Internally we haven't a clue what's happening. Damn that Digger for not leaving Jack's gear with him. He'd have some kind of coagulation drug in it for sure, probably an inhalant.'

'Unless he didn't know he had von Willebrand's. Some people don't, do they?'

Hamish nodded. He was counting respirations. Their patient would make it through the night, he was sure of that. And providing they could stem the infection, he would recover from this wound. What he wasn't sure about was what would happen after that. Lucky was the hospital's miracle baby, but his mother, Megan, and her family had been going through a rough time for years, and now, right when it looked as if things might be coming good for them, Lucky's father could end up in jail.

Hamish looked out into the darkness. Kate's idea of finding the cattle duffers and bringing them to justice was suddenly very appealing.

And very stupid, he admitted to himself, but he turned to study the spunky woman who'd suggested it. She was unfolding a space blanket, her head bent as she concentrated on spreading it out, neat white teeth biting the corner of her lower lip. He saw her again as he'd first seen her, and heard her voice saying 'piffle' in a no-nonsense way to Jack.

You don't fall in love because of a sunbeam turning brown curls golden, or because a husky voice says 'piffle.' But if he wasn't in love then he must be sickening for something. Elevated heart rate, shallow respiration, a slightly nauseous feeling in the pit of his stomach, as if something disagreeable was lurking there—and all this without taking into consideration the stirring in his groin whenever he looked at the woman.

She's not interested, he reminded himself. And who could blame her, after what she's been through? Even if she was interested, she's here on a mission and you're going home in three weeks. Home to a position you've waited two years to secure, home to specialise in paediatrics—your life-long dream-come-true scenario. You cannot fall in love with Kate Winship.

'Here's your blanket. Do you want another of those dreadful biscuits from the provision pack?'

'Those dreadful biscuits are proven to be life-sustaining. They probably contain more nutrition than your regular three meals a day.'

It would be nice to eat three meals a day with Kate…

'But they taste terrible,' Kate reminded him with a smile.

And have her smiling at him all the time…

'Should we take turns to watch him?' She nodded towards their patient.

'I'll doze beside him. I'll need to change the fluid bags during the night, and probably see to fluid output as well. I think he'd prefer I tended him.'

Kate nodded, knowing this was an indication she should move a little further away to give Jack and Hamish privacy, but there was someone out there who might not want Jack rescued.

'Bring the backpack to cushion the rock, and sleep on the other side of me,' Hamish suggested, apparently reading her thoughts with ease. 'I'm big enough to block Jack's view of you, and to shade you from the lamplight. Come on. We'll be warmer if we're all close together.'

Not too close, Kate warned herself, but she lifted the pack and carried it around to Hamish's side of the patient, opening it in the light first so he could get out what he'd need during the night, then pushing it into place against the rock wall.

'I'm not sure that a backpack full of medical supplies makes the perfect pillow,' she said, as she tried to shift box-shaped lumps around inside it.

'Try sleeping against a folded aluminium stretcher,' Hamish countered, but he leaned over and removed some of the boxes from her pack, stacking them neatly on the ledge. 'Better?'

His face was shadowed but she knew he was smiling, because she could hear the amusement in his voice. He was a nice man, she decided—the kind of man a girl would be lucky to meet should she be on the lookout for *nice* in a man.

Or anything in a man.

Or a man…

Was it a sound that had woken her? Hamish must have turned off the lamp, for the cave was dark. Kate lay still, knowing any movement would rustle the silver blanket tucked around her body. Someone—or something—was moving out there.

'Shh!'

She didn't need the barely breathed warning but it was comforting to know Hamish was awake—comforting to feel his hand find her shoulder and give it a reassuring squeeze.

He'd be a nice man to hug.

Good thing he couldn't see the eye-roll that was her reaction to the stupid thought. She had to get a grip. What she needed was a big rock to hide behind, not a hug. What use were hugs if whatever was out there was a man with a gun?

'Look!'

The soft word made her turn, and there, exposed in the moonlight, was a family of wallabies.

'Rock wallabies,' Hamish whispered, as the biggest of the three lifted his delicately shaped head and looked around, scenting some alien presence in his domain. The middle one was also curious, but anxious about the youngster, who was braver in his exploration of the world. Kate sighed at the wonder of it.

'I didn't know they were nocturnal,' she murmured, fascinated by the threesome who had paused, as if posed for photographs, right in front of her.

'It's nearly dawn. They'll feed now until the sun gets too hot then rest in the shade for the remainder of the day.'

A shot rang out, then echoed frighteningly back at them again and again. Two of the wallabies had disappeared, but the third lay still in front of them, the long back legs twitching one or twice.

'That's Todd! He's out there. It's a warning.'

Jack's voice quivered with fear, and Hamish's 'Get back here' was far louder, but Kate was already bending over the injured wallaby, trying to turn the body to see the wound. Then she was lifted from the ground and carried back into the cave.

'You stupid woman! He had a clear shot at the 'roo from wherever he was and you go out there and make a bigger target for him. Are you insane?'

'It might not be dead.'

Kate couldn't believe the dampness on her cheeks could possibly be tears. She hadn't cried when Bill had told her she'd been fostered. She hadn't cried when she'd found out about Daniel and Lindy. She hadn't even cried when she'd discovered she'd missed meeting her birth mother by one lousy week—so why was she crying over a dead animal?

'We'll check later.' Hamish was still holding her, but more gently now, brushing his hand over her head and repeating the words as if he knew she needed the reassurance. 'We'll check when we hear the chopper overhead. If it's only injured we can take it out with us, but experienced 'roo shooters shoot to kill, Kate.'

'He'll shoot us all.' Jack's panic reminded Kate she had a patient to tend. She pushed away from Hamish, swiped her hands across her face and knelt beside the young man, who was frantically trying to free himself from tubes and bags of fluid.

'He's just trying to scare us,' Hamish said, but his Scottish accent didn't make the words any less ridiculous.

'Well, he's succeeded in that part of his plan. What's next?' Kate muttered, holding tightly to Jack's hand—finding as much comfort as she was giving.

'I doubt he wants three bodies on his hands. It's not as if he has the luxury of time to get rid of any trace of us. Having heard the chopper yesterday, he'll know it will be coming back for us at first light. I'd say the gunshot was a warning to Jack not to talk about what's been going on.'

'As if I would!' Jack muttered, and though Kate wanted to argue with him he was still feverish and they had a difficult time ahead of them, getting him safely out of the gorge.

Which reminded her.

'Did you find an open space we can use to winch Jack up?' she asked Hamish, though the thought of how vulnerable they'd be when they left the cave, she and Hamish carrying the stretcher, Jack strapped to it between them, made her shiver.

'I did, and not too far away. It's getting lighter by the minute, so Rex will be on his way. Once he's overhead we'll have radio contact with him and I'll let him know there's some unfriendly person out there. He'll buzz around and hover over us when we move, but I'm sure this Todd person fired his shot to frighten Jack, then took off.'

'I should have died. You should have let me die!' Jack said, and Kate rounded on him.

'If you moan like that once more I swear I'll finish you off myself. Think of it as a big adventure in your path to adulthood. As a great story you can tell your kids in the future. How many young men your age have been shot at and had to huddle in a cave in a gorge in the middle of nowhere, and been rescued by…' She turned to Hamish. 'Could we be Batman and Robin, do you think? Swooping out of the sky in our Bat Helicopter?'

She looked up at Hamish. 'Bags I be Batman!'

Hamish was kneeling on the floor of the cave, fitting the long sides of the stretcher together. He turned towards her and smiled.

'And that would make me Robin?'

'Or Jack could be Robin and you could be the butler guy who answered the phone at the mansion.'

'That's not very fair,' Hamish protested, moving the now-assembled stretcher over to their patient. 'I flew in too so I have to be Robin.'

'I don't need that. I can walk—or hop—if the two of you support me,' Jack protested. He sat up to prove his point, and as the colour faded from his cheeks Kate caught him and rested him gently back against the pillow.

'Not just yet,' she said, helping Hamish position the stretcher where they needed it. 'It's far easier to carry you if you're lying down, and much safer winching you up in a stretcher harness. I imagine Hamish will go first so he can get you safely inside, then you, then I'll follow.'

She glanced up to see Hamish frowning at her.

'It's the only practical way to do it,' she pointed out, though she knew he'd know it. It was the knight errantry thing again—he didn't want her down here on her own. 'I'll be fine—I'm Batman, remember.'

Her reward was a brief smile, flashing across his tired, unshaven face, but the smile was almost immediately replaced by a new frown.

'Just remember Batman wasn't indestructible,' he warned,

then he turned his attention to Jack, explaining how they would move him onto the stretcher.

'When it's time to move, we'll take you off the oxygen and stop the IV fluid until you're on board. The fewer tubes you have around you, the less likely it is we'll foul the winch ropes.'

'Boy, that's a comforting thing to be telling a patient,' Kate remarked, fitting a strap across Jack's chest. 'Less likely to foul the winch ropes! And just how often does this service have trouble with winch ropes?'

'Never in my time,' Hamish reassured Jack, then he smiled again at Kate. 'But I believe when it does happen, it's usually on the third lift.'

'Great! Might have known!' she said, poking Jack's arm with her finger. 'Told you my life was worse than yours.'

Hamish studied her for a moment, and saw the small even teeth once again nibbling at the corner of her lower lip as she fastened the straps on the stretcher. She must be scared stiff, but she was dealing with it her way—with teasing humour. He wasn't exactly unconcerned himself. Dangling on the end of a winch rope, all three of them in turn would make perfect targets for a man with a rifle.

Hamish could tell himself any shooting at this stage would bring the full might of the Queensland police into the gorge, so the man called Todd would be stupid to take aim at any of them.

But believing it was harder.

How badly did Todd want to protect his secret?

How far would he go?

CHAPTER THREE

IN THE END, the airlift was completed safely, though delayed for several hours, Rex insisting the three on the ground remain in their cave until the rescue helicopter from Townsville arrived with armed police. Two of this contingent, carrying serious 'don't mess with us' rifles, were lowered to the ground to escort Jack, Hamish and Kate to the retrieval area. The second helicopter then flew surveillance while Hamish, the patient and finally Kate were winched aboard the Crocodile Creek chopper.

'Now everyone in the whole world knows I'm in trouble,' Jack muttered to Kate an hour later, as he was lifted from the helicopter at Crocodile Creek, TV news cameras capturing the scene.

'I doubt the *whole* world will know,' Kate retorted. 'North Queensland maybe, if it's a slow news day, but this kind of footage never makes the national news. They're taking it for a local station.'

'Big deal,' Jack grumbled. 'Both my mother's brothers are locals.'

He closed his eyes as he had done back in the cave, and Kate, tired as she was, felt a wave of sympathy for him. She took his hand. 'It will be OK,' she promised. 'We'll work it out. You're not on your own, you know. Even if your family is upset with you, Hamish and I will stick by you.'

Having made this promise on Hamish's behalf, she glanced

around. The man in question had spoken briefly to the two orderlies who'd met the chopper, then walked away. Ah, there he
was—over on the edge of the gathered crowd, squatting down
so he could speak in confidence to a man in a wheelchair.

Still holding Jack's hand, she was moving further and
further away from the pair, and as they approached the hospital
she felt a sense of... Surely it wasn't loss? No way. She hardly
knew the man, so why should he stick around? Escort her into
the hospital? Introduce her around?

Because he seemed so nice, that's why.

You don't need nice, she reminded herself, dredging up a
smile for a good-looking man with burnt red curls who was
coming towards them now.

'You must be Kate!' the man said, holding out his hand
towards her, though she knew most of his attention was on Jack.
'I'm Cal Jamieson, the surgeon who'll be digging the bullet out
of your patient's leg.'

He introduced himself to Jack and gave directions for the
orderlies to take him into the emergency department first. The
men wheeled their charge onto a wide veranda, turning right
and entering through a door into a long, bright room, with
curtains hanging from ceiling racks to divide off cubicles.

Kate undid the straps and the orderlies lifted Jack onto an
examination table.

'We'll take a good look at it here,' Cal explained to Jack,
then he looked across at Kate. 'You can stay if you want—meet
some of the staff—but I imagine a shower and a sleep might
be more of a priority.'

'Is that a tactful way of telling me I'm on the nose?' Kate lifted
her arm and sniffed at her T-shirt. Not too bad, considering.

Cal laughed.

'Definitely not. I just know how those overnighters can be.'

'Stay with me, Kate.' Jack decided for her. 'You promised.'

'I didn't promise to stay with you for ever and ever,' she told him firmly. 'But just for now, I will. Until Dr Jamieson puts you under for the op. Then I'll go home and shower and be back when you wake up. That's if I'm not rostered on duty.'

'I think they'll let you have the rest of today to yourself,' Cal said. 'And here's someone who can confirm that. Jill Shaw, Director of Nursing, meet Kate Winship, new nurse and local heroine.'

'I'm not a heroine!'

Kate's protest cut across Jill's quiet, 'How do you do, and a belated welcome to Crocodile Creek.'

Jill held out her hand, and as Kate shook it she sensed a quiet strength in the older woman. Here was someone, she knew immediately, who would stand firm in crises, and who would be there for her staff should they ever need her.

'We were giving you today to settle in,' she said, confirming Cal's words. 'And tomorrow we thought you might like to go on the clinic run to Wygera, so you can see a bit of the countryside and meet some of the people out there.'

Kate opened her mouth to ask about this place, but Jill was already bent over Jack, talking quietly to him. Did she know him?

'Uncle Charles'll kill me!' Jack protested, and Kate realised Hamish's surmises had been correct.

'Don't overdo the drama,' Jill said, but she was smiling fondly at the young man. 'Besides, his job is to save people from death, not cause it. You're in trouble, yes, but Charles and Philip will both stand by you. You should know that.'

'Charles might, but Philip certainly won't,' Jack muttered.

'I think we should get this bullet out of your leg and worry about who kills who later,' Cal said. He nodded towards a young woman who'd wheeled an X-ray machine into the room. 'Right thigh, top and side views. Everyone out.'

Kate gave Jack's hand an extra squeeze and left the cubicle.

'He's really worried about the repercussions of whatever he's been up to,' she said to Jill.

'He should be,' Jill replied, frowning in the direction of the wounded young man. 'Hamish radioed Charles from the helicopter. Cattle duffing—if that's what he's been involved in— is a serious business up here—anywhere in outback Australia really. The sentences and fines have recently been increased. Oh, here's Charles now.'

Kate looked around to find the man in the wheelchair had silently joined them.

'I believe I owe you a debt of gratitude,' he said. He, too, held out his hand. 'Charles Wetherby.'

'Kate Winship,' Kate replied. 'And no gratitude required. I was only doing my job.'

'And doing it very well, from what I hear,' Charles told her, a warm smile lighting up his craggy face. 'Thanks, Kate. I haven't seen much of young Jack lately, but as a kid he often holidayed up here and I'm very fond of him. I didn't know he was at Wetherby Downs let alone that he'd fallen out with Philip and left. Silly young ass—he should have known he could come here. I'd have found him another job somewhere in the area.'

'He might have thought you'd side with your brother.' Hamish's voice made Kate look up to find he'd come in through another door and was standing behind Jill. Kate smiled at him, then realised she shouldn't have. Not that smiles meant anything. Not hers, nor the warm, friendly one Hamish bestowed on her in return. 'Now, Kate, shouldn't you have returned to your unpacking and settling in?'

'I promised Jack I'd stay until he goes to Theatre,' Kate told him, and Charles laughed.

'I notice Jill's standing guard over him as well. The young rascal wormed his way into her heart when he was a kid, always heading for her place if he was in trouble with me or his grandmother.'

Kate wished Jack could hear the affection in Charles's voice as he spoke of his nephew. Jack's fears he'd be disinherited were obviously baseless. She was relieved for him, of course, but somehow it made her own aloneness more acute.

And her desire to find her father even stronger—her father and perhaps some other family. Both her parents—the ones she'd known—had been only children, in their forties when they had taken Kate in, so though she'd known and loved her mother's father, there were no other relatives.

'The wound's infected but the X-rays don't show any nasty surprises, apart from a groove along part of his femur and some serious blood pooling further up around his hip.' Cal appeared from the curtained cubicle to deliver his good news. 'I want to get the clotting time down in his blood. I've got cryoprecipi-tate running into him now in a rapid infusion, and I'll give Alix more blood to test when that's done. I spoke to a haematolo-gist after Hamish radioed in and described the patient, and Charles confirmed it was his nephew. The haematologist says minor surgery is OK once we get the blood-clotting factors up to thirty per cent of normal. The cryoprecipitate should do that.'

'Do you want us to thaw some FFP just in case?' Charles asked, and Kate realised just how sophisticated this country hospital was, to have fresh frozen plasma on hand.

Cal thought for a moment.

'It's such a waste to thaw it if we don't need it within twenty-four hours. What's thawing time?'

'Twenty minutes.'

An attractive young woman with a long plait of dark hair swinging down her back answered the question as she came briskly into the room. She nodded at Kate then turned to Cal.

'His clotting time is up to fifty per cent of normal. You can go ahead.'

'Thanks, Alix.'

Cal disappeared back behind the curtain.

'Alix, this is Kate. Kate Winship, meet our pathologist, Alix Armstrong.'

'Hi,' Alix said. 'You've had an exciting introduction to Crocodile Creek. I'd love to hear about the gorge some time, but right now I need to talk to Cal about what he'll need in Theatre.'

'Alix is bush-crazy,' Charles explained to Kate. 'All her time off is spent bush-walking. She's serious about wanting to hear about the gorge.'

Kate shivered, memories of the echoing gunshot sending icy tentacles along her spine.

Had Hamish noticed, that he put his hand lightly on her shoulder?

'I'd better go in and see Jack before he goes to Theatre,' she said, moving away from Hamish as swiftly as she could, but Charles was before her, shifting the curtain aside and wheeling silently towards the bed. He reached out and touched Jack's cheek with the back of his hand.

'Silly young fool,' he said gruffly, and Kate swallowed hard. It wasn't that she begrudged Jack this familial affection, just that once again it emphasised her own lack.

She took Jack's hand, promised to see him later and left the cubicle, assuring herself it was lack of sleep and a letdown after the tension of the night that was making her so stupidly sentimental.

A small boy who looked just like Cal was sitting on the top step when she arrived back at the house. Beside him, spreadeagled like a fireside rug, was the weirdest dog Kate had ever seen. Part cocker spaniel and part something spotty, she guessed, greeting both boy and dog with a smile.

'Hello, I'm Kate. Who are you two?'

'I'm CJ and this is Rudolph, and his nose isn't red because he's not called after a reindeer but after a dancing man. I'm hiding.'

'I thought you might be,' Kate said easily. 'From anyone in particular?'

'I'm supposed to be at that stupid child-care place, but Rudolph followed me and sat outside so I decided to take him home, and he won't stay home on his own so I'm here, too.'

'Of course,' Kate said, not understanding much of the conversation. 'Do you think the people who mind you at the child-care place will be worried?'

'They won't notice 'cos they don't know me 'cos I'm new. Or they might think I'm sick.'

'Well, that's OK, then,' Kate said, climbing the steps and sitting beside the pair.

Rudolph raised his dopey head and soft brown eyes looked deep into hers, then he dropped his head onto her leg and went back to sleep. Going to child care and back must have been a tiring business.

'I'm waiting for Hamish, he'll know what to do.'

'I'm sure he will,' Kate agreed. This was obviously a job for Robin rather than Batman.

Fortunately, the top of Hamish's dark head appeared above the foliage in the garden, and the dog, perhaps sensing his presence, woke up, then loped off down the steps, the huge grin on his canine face making him look even dopier.

The boy followed the dog, disappearing round a bend in the path then reappearing on Hamish's shoulders, the dog lolloping around his legs.

'You've met CJ, then?' Hamish greeted her, and Kate nodded. 'He's absconded from child care again,' Hamish continued, apparently unperturbed by the child's delinquency.

He set CJ back down on the top step, then sat himself down in the space between the child and Kate. Rudolph found this unacceptable and proceeded to spread himself over all three of them.

'Off! Sit!' Hamish ordered, and the dog looked at him in surprise, then, to Kate's astonishment, obeyed.

'I've been teaching him to sit, like you told me,' CJ said, giving the dog a big hug and kiss. 'He's a very clever dog, isn't he?'

'Yes, he is,' Hamish told him. 'It's just a pity he's going to have to go and live somewhere else.'

'But he can't go somewhere else to live,' CJ protested. 'He's *my* dog!'

He gathered an armful of dog to his chest as he spoke, and glared at Hamish over the spotty head.

Hamish nodded.

'He is, but if he keeps causing trouble, like making you run away from child care, your mom will just have to give him away.'

Silence, and Kate, who thought Hamish's chiding had been unnecessarily harsh, reached around behind his back to pat CJ on the arm.

'They laugh at me.'

The whispered words were barely audible, but understandable enough to make Kate's stomach clench.

Hamish, however, seemed unmoved.

'Who?'

'Some of the kids. They say I talk funny.'

'Bloody kids,' Kate muttered under her breath. OK, so CJ appeared to have a slight American accent, but did that make him so different? At child-care level? What age would the kids be? Four? Five at the most?

'Of course you do—that's because you're half-American— and it's not funny, it's just an accent, like mine is. But kids love to pick on anyone who seems different. The trick is to ignore them and eventually they'll get tired of it and pick on someone else.'

'Then that someone will be sad,' CJ pointed out, and Kate glanced at Hamish, wondering how he'd handle that one.

'Why don't you make your difference count?' he suggested, ignoring the bit Kate had wondered about. 'Think of all the great things that have come from the United States of America—spaceships and astronauts and all the movies those kids at school go to see, not to mention most of the television they watch, and X-Boxes and video games.'

'Could I tell them my father was an astronaut?' he asked, and Kate looked at the burnt red curls and raised her eyebrows at Hamish.

'It's complicated,' Hamish said in an aside to her, before tackling CJ's question.

'I wouldn't tell a lie,' he said mildly. 'Lies are hard because you have to remember what you said the first time you told it, and then they grow bigger and bigger and it all gets very complicated. But you could tell them that you're going to be an astronaut when you grow up, and you could take spaceship stuff along to child care to show them.'

'I don't have any spaceship stuff.'

Kate smiled. The kid had Hamish now.

'Cal will help you make some,' he said. 'Cal knows all kinds of things about space and the solar system and other solar systems. You ask him to help you.'

CJ considered this for a moment, then he nodded.

'He does know a lot of stuff. I like Cal. But he's working and so's Mom, so would you take me back and tell the teacher I was late because the man with the gun made the helicopter late?'

Hamish sighed.

'I'll take you back to child care and tell the teacher you had trouble getting Rudolph to stay home,' he said. 'Remember what I told you about lies?'

CJ nodded, and lifted one of Rudolph's silky ears.

'I'd like child care a whole lot better if he could come with me.'

The wistful statement made Kate smile, but Hamish was getting to his feet, giving orders for Rudolph to stay and sending CJ to wash his hands and face before they departed.

'Mom, Dad, Cal?' Kate asked him, when the boy had disappeared.

'I'll explain later,' Hamish promised. 'In the meantime, would you mind seeing that Rudolph doesn't follow us? The dopey dog once chased my car right up the main street of the town, just because I had CJ with me. I'll get his lead—Rudolph's, not CJ's, although maybe he needs one too—and if you can just hold him while we get going, then tell him to stay, he should be OK. The child-care centre is just the other side of the hospital, so I won't be long.'

Hamish disappeared inside the house, reappearing with CJ a few minutes later. He waited patiently while CJ kissed the dog goodbye, clipped on the lead and handed it to Kate, then he herded CJ through the house and out the front door.

Kate shifted from the step to an old settee set back in the shade of the back veranda. Rudolph needed no invitation to climb up and flop beside her.

'Dog-minding duties? I assume you're Kate and no doubt Hamish roped you in to hold that hound.'

A woman with a cascade of deep brown curls and a soft American accent was taking the steps two at a time.

'Is CJ with Hamish? Did Hamish take him back to child care?'

Kate nodded, and the woman pushed the dog to one side and flopped down on the couch.

'I'm Gina,' she said, 'CJ's mother, in case you hadn't guessed. I don't think it's the child-care place that's bothering CJ so much as not being here. From the day we arrived, he's been petted and spoilt by everyone in the hospital, so now he thinks he might be missing out on something if he's not here. What was his excuse this morning?'

Kate stared at the woman who was frowning at the spectacular view beyond the garden.

'He had to bring the dog home,' Kate offered, and Gina gave a scoffing laugh.

'This dog could find his way to Mars if he had to,' she said, patting the head of the dog in question with absent-minded affection. 'I keep wondering if it's because of Cal. CJ's more or less had me to himself since my husband died, and now he has to share me with Cal, but he seems to love Cal and the two did boy things together all weekend, so…'

She sighed, then added, 'I don't know! Perhaps I should stop work and be a full-time mother, though I know I'd hate not working and the hospital needs a cardiologist.'

She stopped again, and flashed a smile at Kate.

'Heavens, but you're good! You arrive here and get whisked away on a rescue mission, then get shot at, then left to mind a dog, and now some total stranger is unloading on you—and you're just sitting there and taking it. Tell me to go get a life!'

Kate smiled at her vehemence.

'I'm really too tired to tell anyone to do anything,' she admitted. 'I'd be inside sleeping only once I go to sleep I might not wake for twenty-four hours and I promised Jack—the young man we brought in—I'd be there when he comes out of Theatre, so I may as well be dog-minding and listening to anyone who wants to unload.'

Gina reached across the dog and gave her a hug.

'Thanks,' she said. 'But now I know CJ's gone back—one of the carers rings me as soon as they realise he'd done a bunk. Problem is, they can't work out how he gets out, with the child-proof locks on the gates. Anyway, that's my problem, or theirs, really, because they have to stop it happening. For now, this mongrel…' she brushed his ears with loving hands '…can be shut on the side veranda, so why don't you have a shower and lie down? I promise I'll come over and wake you when Jack comes out of Theatre. Have you got a room? Did you get that far when you arrived?'

'I have and I did, but I haven't unpacked. Maybe I will have a shower and unpack, then see about a sleep.'

Kate looked anxiously at Gina.

'You *will* wake me?'

'Promise!' Gina said, then she took the lead from Kate. 'Cal and I have a kind of flat on the hospital side of the house,' she explained. 'There are two of them—ours is two-bedroom and the other is a one-bedroom. Mike and Emily are using the other one, though not for long. Mike's parents are building a place for them beside their house and restaurant on the other side of the cove.'

'You and Cal, Mike and Emily—is this pairing off to do with the love epidemic Hamish said was happening in Crocodile Creek?'

Gina laughed.

'I guess you could call it that. You're lucky Christina and Joe are over in New Zealand, or you'd have three pairs of love-birds under your feet.'

Kate looked at the still smiling woman, seeing the translu-cence of love in her eyes and the sheer delight of it in her smile. Gina might be worried about her son settling into the child-care centre, but there was no doubt the rest of her life was richly rewarding right now.

'See you later,' Gina added, leading Rudolph away along the veranda.

Kate stayed where she was for a little longer, then decided she really, really needed a shower, and if she didn't get up and have one right now, she'd fall asleep on the settee and be there until nightfall.

She found the room she'd been allotted, and was surprised to see her case had been unpacked, her clothes hung in the wardrobe and her toiletries set out on a small dressing-table. A plastic folder on the bed held a plan of the house, the rooms or suites marked with the occupants' names, while the kitchen had a note beside it, giving the times breakfast and dinner were served at the staff dining room at the hospital should the tenants not want to cook.

A second sheet of paper showed a plan of the downstairs

area of the old house. This was obviously the rec room—with a bar, pool table and a big-screen TV marked. Below that was a note explaining when and where laundry could be left, and a phone number for her to contact someone called Dora Grubb, should she need any more information.

A place like this, she realised, with resident doctors and nurses working irregular hours, would need someone to keep it running, and from the look of the spotless room Kate had been given, Mrs Grubb did a wonderful job.

Kate set the folder aside, noting as she did so that the closest bathroom was two doors down the central passageway. Gathering up what she needed, she headed straight there. Suddenly a shower seemed infinitely appealing, but she'd get dressed again after it and sleep in her clothes, knowing Gina could return to wake her any time.

Hamish knocked, then opened the door very quietly. Kate was sleeping soundly, fully clothed but with a throw across her legs. He'd called in at the hospital after dropping CJ back at the child-care centre, and Gina, after thanking him for his help, had asked him to wake Kate and tell her Jack was about to be shifted to Recovery.

She couldn't have been asleep very long, he knew that, but he also knew she'd want to keep her promise to Jack.

'Kate!'

Not wanting to enter her room, he called her name from the doorway, but when she didn't stir he ventured inside, telling himself that looking at a sleeping woman wasn't really voyeurism. Yet looking at her disturbed him and he finally nailed the reason. It was something to do with the total vulnerability of a sleeping woman—anyone asleep, he supposed, though he doubted he'd get knots in his stomach watching Cal sleep.

'Kate! Wake up.'

He put his hand on her shoulder and shook her gently,

watching her eyes snap open, her expression confused at first then clearing as the dark brown irises focussed on him. Her full lips curved into a smile.

'Jack's awake?'

She sat up, dropped her legs off the side of the bed and thrust her feet into the flowery purple sandals. 'Thanks for waking me.'

That was it? *Thanks for waking me?* Well, what had he expected? Sleeping Beauty after the Prince's kiss?

Weird thoughts were still muddling around in his head while Kate pulled a brush through her loose curls, dropped it back on the dressing-table then left the room, poking her head back inside a moment later.

'I think you've done enough good deeds for the day, Dr McGregor. Go have a sleep.'

Hamish looked down at Kate's bed, still with the indentation of her body on it, and thought of his own bed awaiting him next door. An urge to lie on her bed—feel the warmth of where she'd been—was so strong he very nearly gave in to it. After all, he'd heard her sandals tap-tap-tap their way along the hall and through the kitchen to the back steps. She'd be well on her way to the hospital by now.

Then, shaking his head at the folly of his thoughts, he left the room. A shower and a sleep would surely sort him out. Tiredness, that was all it was, not love at all.

CHAPTER FOUR

A TALL POLICEMAN with cool grey eyes and floppy black hair was leaning against the wall in the ED when Kate entered it, looking for someone to give her directions to Recovery. He smiled at her and she found herself returning the smile, though this probably wasn't an occasion to ask a policeman for directions.

A nurse with a badge that said her name was Grace appeared from inside a cubicle, and flashed another smile in Kate's direction.

'Recovery is through that door, down the corridor, turn left and it's the first door on your right,' she said.

'Am I the only stranger in town, that everyone seems to know who I am?' Kate asked.

'The only small, dark curly-haired stranger at the hospital,' Grace told her, then she introduced herself. 'Actually, Harry here is waiting to see Jack as well. You could take him with you if you like.'

Kate looked up at the policeman. He was no longer smiling but neither was she.

'You want to see him right now? He'll be in terrible shape, just out of an op. Is that fair, talking to him when he'll be woozy as all get out?'

'Probably not,' the policeman called Harry said. 'But there's someone out there with a gun and, as far as we can tell, he's not too fussy about where, when or at whom he points and fires it. The sooner we have information about him, the safer it will be for anyone in his vicinity.'

Kate couldn't argue with the theory, but in practice, if this man tried to badger Jack...

She followed Grace's directions, very aware of the man walking beside her. A local policeman—if he was a local—could be very useful in her search for information about her birth parents, so perhaps she shouldn't antagonise him.

Like hell she shouldn't. Jack was her patient—kind of—and she wasn't about to allow this policeman to bother him.

'Are you a local?' she asked, as they turned the corner and she saw the recovery room in front of them.

'Born and bred,' he said, pushing open the door and holding it for her. 'My family have owned the sugar mill here for generations.'

So he *would* be useful.

But Jack wasn't only physically unwell, he was emotionally upset. He was also awake, and looking around. A pretty woman with honey blonde hair and grey-blue eyes was on the other side of the bed, studying the monitors to which Jack was still attached.

'Hi, I'm Emily,' she said, barely turning her attention from the screen in front of her.

Kate nodded in response then hurried forward, taking Jack's hand and holding it in both of hers.

'I thought you weren't coming,' he said, and Kate saw the tears in his eyes.

'You came out of that anaesthetic far faster than I thought you would,' she told him. 'You are one tough guy.'

The tears were blinked away and he smiled, then must have noticed Harry standing right behind her, for he paled and closed his eyes.

But before Harry could ask questions, the cavalry arrived. Charles wheeled himself into the room, Jill and Cal not far behind.

'Sorry, Harry, but we need you out of here.' There was no mistaking the authority in Charles's voice. 'The surgery's shown up an unexpected complication. We need scans and more blood tests and some expert advice on what to do next. I'm expecting he'll need to go back into Theatre today, or tomorrow at the latest. Kate, Cal will fill you in on what's happening—Cal, take Kate through to the dining room for a coffee. Jill and I will stay with Jack until you get back.'

Harry left without an argument, but what surprised Kate even more was Jack's acceptance of the orders. Here she was, being hustled down the corridor by Cal, and Jack hadn't even protested.

'Did Charles do that to prevent the policeman questioning Jack just yet, or is there a problem?' she asked Cal.

'Big problem,' Cal said gloomily. 'Big, big problem. Here.'

He directed her in through a door into a reasonably sized dining room, where the smell of coffee and the enticing aroma of a hot meal reminded Kate it had been a long time since she'd eaten the dreadful dry biscuits.

'Do you want food? There's always something hot in the bains-marie along that side, and cold sandwiches and salads in the fridge.'

It was closer to dinnertime than lunch, but Kate chose a pack of salad sandwiches while Cal fixed their coffee. They were heading for a table at one side of the room when Hamish appeared.

'Problems?' he said, raising his eyebrows at Cal this time.

'And then some. Did you find out about it through osmosis?'

Hamish grinned and slipped into a chair between Cal and Kate.

'Much the same thing. Mrs Grubb. She came over to make sure there was food in the house for me and Kate and told me Harry Blake had been turned away from questioning Jack in Recovery because of some complication.'

Cal sighed.

'The bullet is lodged in bone. The X-ray wasn't clear because there was a lot of blood pooled around the actual site, and when I went in I could see the bullet had scored down along the periosteum.' Cal turned to Kate. 'That's the fibrous vascular membrane that covers bones. Then it entered the greater trochanter.'

'The ball-shaped head of the femur that fits into the hip bone?' Kate checked.

'A job for an orthopod?' Hamish asked.

Cal nodded.

'Which means flying Jack out to Townsville,' Hamish said.

Cal shook his head. 'Charles doesn't want to do that. He says we have all we need here, and the flight could further weaken the lad. He *is* very sick—the infection is still causing fever—but I think that's just an excuse. Damn, but it's complicated!'

Cal stirred sugar into his coffee then tapped the teaspoon fretfully on the side of the cup.

'I suppose Charles is worried that if Jack goes to Townsville and the police there become involved, Jack could be placed under arrest,' Hamish suggested, taking the teaspoon out of Cal's hand and setting it on the table.

'Placed under arrest? Why?' Kate demanded. 'He hasn't confessed to anything. All we know is that he's been shot. The rest is just guesswork.'

'No, Hamish is right. That's a definite possibility. Apparently there's been a special federal police squad working on organised cattle thefts in this area,' Cal explained. 'One of their officers went under cover some months ago, and only last week his body was found—in a state of advanced decomposition and with a bullet in his chest. If that bullet matches the one in Jack's leg, it's enough of a connection for the police to hold him pending further enquiries.'

'But he was the one who was shot, not the shooter,' Kate protested, looking at Hamish as she recalled the saga he'd told her. 'And what about Megan and Lucky and Mr Cooper? What will it do to Mr Cooper's fragile health if his grandson's father is arrested?'

Hamish shrugged his shoulders.

'I'm sure Charles is considering all of that,' Cal told them. 'He probably feels he might have more control over the situation if we keep Jack here and Harry does the investigation. But there's more to it than the police side of things. First, the kid's Charles's nephew and Charles will want to keep an eye on him. It was a dumb accident with a gun when he was a kid that put Charles in a wheelchair and I'm betting there are a whole bunch of memories being stirred up right now that Charles is trying to keep a lid on. Charles's accident caused the family feud which is maybe how Jack got to be in this mess. So Charles is going to want to hold him close.'

'But doesn't Jack have parents? Do they have a say in this?' Kate asked.

'That's the next hassle,' Cal explained. 'Charles has to let them know he's injured, and if they hear we're moving him to another hospital, Charles believes they'll want him flown to Sydney—to top specialists down there.'

'But if he's in Sydney and Megan's up here, what chance will they have to sort out their feelings for each other?'

Cal answered Kate's new protest with a nod.

'Exactly!' he said. 'That's the other reason we really need to keep him here if we possibly can.'

'So, what's the answer?' Hamish asked Cal. 'Will you do the op? Do you feel confident of handling it?'

Cal hesitated.

'With expert help, yes. Charles is trying to set it up now. He has a friend, an orthopaedic surgeon, in Brisbane. If we set up a video camera and link it via computer to Charles's mate, he can virtually guide my hands. In a less complicated form, this system's being trialled in a number of country areas where there's a nurse but no doctor. It's mainly been used for diagnostic purposes but some operations have been performed this way.'

'You OK with it?' Hamish asked, and Kate sensed a bond between the two men.

Cal nodded.

'The worst part will be the timing. The surgeon we need is in Theatre right now, and he has a full list for today. It could be midnight before we get going.'

'Late night for all the staff. Because of the von Willebrand's you'll need Alix on hand and Emily for the anaesthetic—do you want me to assist?' Hamish asked.

Cal grinned at him.

'You'll probably be more useful as a babysitter. Knowing Gina, she'll insist on assisting. I know it's not heart surgery, but as soon as she heard you'd found Lucky's father, she's been itching to get involved.'

Kate was only half listening to the conversation, aware more of the interaction of the two men and the sense of belonging that being part of a hospital staff engendered. Dangerous stuff—belonging. She finished her sandwiches, drained her coffee-cup and stood up.

'Speaking of babysitting, I'd better get back to Jack,' she said, and if Hamish looked surprised by her abrupt departure, that was too bad. She'd opted to go through an agency to get this job, rather than applying direct to the hospital. She knew from experience with agency nurses in the hospital in Melbourne that they worked set contracts. They came, they did their jobs, remaining uninvolved with the people around them because they were moving on. Her contract was for two months. Long enough, she'd decided, to find out what she wanted—needed—to know. Then she'd move on.

Yes, she wanted to find her father, and to learn the circumstances of her birth—she needed to know these things to give her new life some foundation. But her new life would not be dependent on other people. From now on, she was depending solely on herself.

'He's sleeping, and so should you be,' Charles told her, when she arrived in Recovery where Jack was being held awaiting his second operation.

'I feel I should stay,' she said, but Jill, on the other side of Jack's bed, shook her head.

'I'll order you to bed if I need to,' she said, smiling to soften the words. 'But common sense should tell you, you need to sleep.'

Kate nodded her agreement but as she walked away she wondered why she felt a little lost now Jack had so many other people to be there for him. This wasn't how someone who depended solely on herself should be feeling.

She made her way back to the house, pleased Hamish was still over at the hospital with Cal, then, as she heard voices in the kitchen, contrarily wished he was here so she wouldn't have to face a roomful of strangers alone.

'Here she is—the elected judge,' someone said, and Kate looked helplessly around the smiling faces, catching sight, eventually, of Gina's.

And CJ's.

CJ and Rudolph and another little boy were cutting and pasting something in a corner where the kitchen opened onto the back veranda.

'Elected judge?' Kate echoed weakly. What on earth were they talking about?

Gina took pity on her, coming forward and introducing her to Mike—the paramedic chopper pilot Hamish had spoken of—and Marcia, a fellow nurse. There was also Susie, a pretty woman with short blonde curly hair and blue eyes who was apparently the hospital physiotherapist, and Georgie Turner, O and G specialist, a stunning young woman with very short shiny black hair and long legs encased in skin-tight jeans. The only other man there was someone called Brian—someone

Kate realised she should have met earlier, as apparently he was the hospital administrator.

'Poor Kate, I bet she doesn't even know about Wygera and the swimming pool,' Georgie said. 'And here we are appointing her judge of the designs.'

'Judge of the designs? I'm a nurse, not an architect.'

The others all chuckled.

'We don't need an architect—well, not yet. We need an unbiased person, someone who doesn't know any of the people of Wygera, to choose the best model or design then we'll pass it on to an architect to draw up the plans for us.'

Kate was about to protest that surely the architect should be the judge when Susie spoke.

'We've been arguing about it for ages, then decided you'd be the best, not only because you don't know anyone and can't be accused of bias but because you're going out there tomorrow. Doing the clinic run. Jill always puts new nurses on the clinic run to give them an idea of the area we cover.'

As everyone was smiling encouragingly at Kate, she couldn't argue, so she accepted the dubious honour of being the judge of the Wygera Swimming Pool Competition.

'Is there a prize? Do I have to give someone something?' she asked, sitting down in the chair Mike had brought over for her.

'The prize is free entry to the rodeo for the entrant and his or her family—within reason, the family part,' Mike explained. 'The company who brings a truck to all the rodeos, selling clothes and rodeo equipment, is also donating a western shirt and hat, so whoever wins gets that as well.'

'We want to win the hat,' a small voice said, and Kate turned to see CJ looking up from his task. 'I've got a hat, but Max hasn't.'

'Max is mine,' Georgie explained, but then everyone was talking again—this time about the barbeque they were planning for dinner—so Kate couldn't ask on what criteria she should judge the contest.

'Are there rules for this contest? I don't want to choose some stupendous design whoever's paying for this pool can't afford.'

'We're paying for the pool,' Georgie said, and Kate looked around the group, arguing amiably about who would do what for the barbeque. None of them looked as if they had fortunes tucked away.

'We're running fundraising events like the rodeo,' Brian explained, 'and soliciting donations from local businesses. The local council has guaranteed to match us on a dollar-for-dollar basis so I think we can afford to build something fairly special.'

Kate smiled to herself. The 'fairly' in front of special showed Brian up as a number-cruncher. Hospital administrators had to be cautious in their spending—after all, it was their job to see the place ran within its means.

The group had by now delegated tasks, and were scattering in various directions, although Gina, Susie and Marcia remained in the kitchen, pulling things out of an old refrigerator and starting work on salads.

'Can I help?' Kate asked, but once again Brian had spoken over her, offering to show her around the hospital, saying they may as well get her paperwork in order.

Kate's apologetic smile at Gina was greeted with a grimace, but directed more at Brian, Kate thought. Was he one of those administrators who insisted on all the paperwork being perfect and always up to date? She'd worked with ward secretaries who'd thought paperwork more important than patients, and it had driven her to distraction.

But she followed Brian out of the house—through the front door this time—and across to the hospital, while he talked about bed numbers, and clinic flights, and retrievals, and how expensive these ancillary services were.

'But people living in isolation five hundred miles away can't rely on an ambulance getting to them, surely,' Kate reminded him, and although he nodded agreement, he didn't seem very happy about it.

'Ah, Kate. I was coming to get you. Jill tells me you're off to Wygera tomorrow so I thought I'd show you around.'

Hamish loomed up as Brian was explaining how much it cost to run the emergency department, giving Kate figures per patient per hour that made her mind close completely. Maths had never been her strong point.

So Hamish was a welcome relief—he, at least, would make the grand tour patient-oriented.

Providing she concentrated on what he was saying, not what she was feeling. The feeling stuff was to do with having spent a fraught night together, nothing more. She knew that, but at the same time knew she should be on her guard.

Feelings could be insidious. Creeping in where they were least wanted.

'No, no, we've paperwork to do. You go on back to the house and help the others with the barbeque. I'll bring Kate when we finish here.'

Brian's assertions cut across her thoughts, so it seemed that even if she'd wanted Hamish as her tour guide, she wasn't going to get him.

By the time they'd seen the hospital, met dozens of staff, completed the forms Brian required for insurance purposes and walked back to the house, the party on the back veranda was in full swing. The smell of searing meat hung in the air, while sizzling onions tantalised Kate's taste-buds.

'After a dry biscuit for breakfast and some sandwiches for a meal at afternoon teatime, that certainly smells good,' she said to Brian, who had put his arm around her waist to guide her into the crowd.

Cal was there, so she headed towards him, anxious to know when Jack's operation would take place, only realising who he was with as she drew closer.

'So, seen all you need to of the hospital?' Hamish asked, frowning at a point over her shoulder.

'More than I could take in,' Kate told him, feeling a new touch on her back and realising Brian had followed her. 'It's far bigger than I thought and I'll be getting lost for at least the first week.'

'I'm sure you won't,' Cal said kindly. 'Did you look in on Jack?'

'He was still sleeping and Charles was with him so I didn't go in. When's the op? Have you heard?'

Cal shrugged.

'Between ten and twelve's the best timing we've got so far,' he said. 'Though we should know more by nine when the surgeon in Brisbane is due to start the last patient on his list.'

Brian had moved to her side and was asking if she wanted a drink, and politeness decreed she answer him.

'Something non-alcoholic—I haven't had much sleep,' Kate told him, pleased he would have to move away so she could ask Cal about the operation. But to her astonishment Brian simply turned to Hamish and said, 'Hamish, would you get a squash for Kate?'

Hamish—Cal, too, for that matter—seemed equally surprised, but Hamish moved obediently away, while Brian, perhaps sensing everyone's reaction, explained, 'I don't live here so don't want to be poking around in their kitchen.'

It was an acceptable excuse, yet Kate felt uncomfortable that Brian was sticking to her like Velcro. She knew it was probably kindness on his part—after all, she was the new face in this gathering of friends and colleagues—but the discomfort remained.

Although being uncomfortable about Brian was certainly distracting her from thoughts of Hamish.

Setting both aside, she returned to her mission—finding out from Cal what lay ahead for Jack.

'I'm virtually doing a hip replacement. We have prosthetic devices here because we have a visiting orthopaedic surgeon who comes once a quarter, operating in Croc Creek to save the patients travelling to him. It will depend on the damage to the neck of the trochanter. If the bullet is deeply lodged, the orthopod in Brisbane suggests we take if off completely and insert a new-age ceramic replacement and ceramic acetabular socket for it.'

Cal smiled at her.

'Want to watch?'

Kate shuddered.

'I had to do a certain amount of theatre work during my training, but the noise of the saws in orthopaedic work put me off that kind of surgery for life.'

'Besides, she needs to sleep,' Gina put in, arriving with Hamish and the lemon squash. 'She'll need all her wits about her to judge the pool entries tomorrow.'

Hamish handed her the drink, and somehow he and Gina managed to detach Brian from her side. Kate wasn't sure but she felt it had been deliberate, a sense confirmed when, a little later, Gina whispered, 'Brian makes a play for all the new female staff and Hamish felt you might be too polite to escape his tenacious clutches.'

Hamish felt that, did he?

Kate scowled at the man in question who'd moved, with his arm around Brian's shoulders, over to the barbeque. She was about to launch into a 'What right had he to make that decision?' tirade to Gina when she realised that she'd given Hamish that right—had told him she wasn't interested in a re-lationship with anyone.

Gina suggested they find a chair before they were all taken.

'Nothing worse than trying to eat barbequed steak standing up,' she said. 'Besides, if we're sitting down, someone might serve us—saves getting in the queue at the salad table.'

Someone did—Hamish bringing two plates piled high with meat and assorted salads across to where they sat.

'CJ's eating with Max and Georgie, and Cal's nabbed us a table at the end of the veranda,' he said, adding, rather obscurely, 'With only four chairs.'

Gina stood up and moved away immediately, though Kate followed more reluctantly. Hamish was only being kind, she knew that, but his kindness—she was sure it was just that—made her feel warm inside. Actually, quite hot in places.

Funny that kindness could have that effect…

'Oh!'

The table Cal had snagged was beyond the old settee and had the most wonderful view out over the cove. The moon had just risen, so it hung like a slightly squashed golden lantern just above the horizon, spreading a path of light across the sea.

'Nice view?' Cal teased, and Kate shook her head.

'I can't believe it,' she whispered, not wanting to break the spell beauty had cast around her.

'It's what makes Crocodile Creek so special,' Hamish said. 'And what I'll miss when I go home. Although I do have a view of the Firth from my flat, and moons do rise in Scotland, though not in quite the same majestic splendour as these tropical moons.'

'You're going home?'

Kate's question came out far louder than she'd intended it to, and she certainly hadn't meant to sound shocked.

'In less than three weeks.' Cal answered for him. 'And, boy, are we going to miss him. I know Charles has a replacement lined up—several replacements, in fact, because we're down about three doctors and we don't know if Joe and Christina will be back—but we've kind of got used to having a big, useless Scot around the place.'

'Useless? I'll give you useless!' Hamish growled, and the others laughed.

'We thought he'd be useless when he first arrived,' Cal explained. 'He was so polite to everyone, and so correct, and he'd never been in a light plane or a helicopter and didn't trust either of them.'

He smiled at his friend. 'But we brought him up to speed, and now, just when he's become a reasonably useful member of the community, he's going back to cold, dreary Scotland.'

'To specialise in paeds,' Gina added, giving Cal a nudge in the side, 'which is what he's always wanted to do, remember. You should be happy for him, not giving him grief.'

Once again Kate was struck by the warmth and camaraderie between these colleagues and housemates—and once again it emphasised her aloneness.

Or was it the news that Hamish was leaving so soon causing the empty feeling inside her?

Not possible.

She was still debating this when Brian appeared, a plate of food in one hand, cutlery poking out of his pocket and dragging a chair behind him.

'Thought I'd lost you,' he said to Kate, pulling his chair into position between her and Gina. 'Great moon, huh? Maybe we can take a walk up onto the headland when we've finished eating. I often take a walk after dinner. Helps me sleep.'

'I doubt Kate needs a walk to help her sleep,' Hamish said, before Kate could think of a reply. 'We had precious little last night and today she's spent most of her time with Jack.'

Kate looked at Hamish, who appeared to be glaring at Brian, although with Hamish's rather severe features it was hard to tell. But, glaring or not, he was going back to Scotland in a couple of weeks so he couldn't possibly be warning Brian away for his own sake.

Did he not like Brian?

Or was he just genuinely interested in her need for sleep?

Whatever! She felt uncomfortable allowing him to take over her decision-making.

'I'd like a walk after dinner,' she said, more to the table in general than to Brian.

'Oh, good, we'll all go,' Gina said.

Which was how Kate's first evening in Crocodile Creek ended in a moonlit walk over the headland above the house with Brian and Hamish, Cal and Gina, Susie, Marcia, Mike, and Georgie, CJ and Max, while a lolloping, lovable, dopey dog called Rudolph gambolled along beside them.

CHAPTER FIVE

'WHAT DO YOU mean he's gone into shock? What kind of shock? Septic from the infection? Hypovolaemic from the blood loss? He's in hospital—how could they let him go into shock?'

Kate was vaguely aware she was shooting the messenger, but Hamish was right there in front of her, so why not vent her anxiety and distress on him? He was big enough to take it.

She had clambered out of bed while he was explaining why he'd woken her for a second time, and was now pulling a pair of sweats over her skimpy pyjama pants. Thrusting her feet into her sandals, she hurried towards the door.

Hamish didn't move.

'Come on, let's go,' she urged.

'You're going like that?'

She glanced down at the amiable hippo on the T-shirt top of her pyjamas.

'I'm decent, Jack's very ill, why not?'

'No reason,' Hamish said, but he shook his head in a bemused manner and followed her through the quiet house.

Were all the occupants over at the hospital, or were some people actually getting some sleep?

As they walked through the garden, an imminent dawn ghosting the foliage into strange shapes and patterns, Hamish explained. The operation to remove the bullet, with the guidance of the surgeon in Brisbane, had apparently gone well, and no replacement devices had been required. Jack had made the transition to the recovery room safely. Even there, Emily had been pleased with his responses as he'd come out of the anaesthetic, then they'd transferred him to the ICU for monitoring, and everything had gone haywire, his blood pressure dropping, pulse rate rising and his mental state confused and lethargic.

He wanted to die, he kept repeating weakly, then closing his eyes in response to any comment or question.

Desperate with concern—had he made the wrong decision doing the op here?—Charles had paged Hamish, asking him to wake Kate in the hope she might be able to rouse the young man.

'The ICU is through here,' Hamish said, guiding Kate with a hand on her elbow to an area she hadn't explored with Brian.

Talk about state of the art. Many city hospitals Kate had seen would have been pleased to have such a set-up. Five rooms, all monitored from a central desk, but only one of them occupied. Behind the desk, a nurse and Emily frowned at the monitor.

Jack's was the room crowded with people in spite of ICU protocols that discouraged such practices.

'Kate!' Charles greeted her with relief. 'I'm sorry, but we thought if you could speak to him—rouse him. Alix is running new blood tests but as yet we can't find any physical reason for his sudden collapse.'

'He's been through a lot,' Kate reminded him, slipping past the man in the wheelchair to reach the side of Jack's bed and take one limp hand in both of hers.

'Hey, Jack, it's me, Kate. Sorry I was a bit late getting here, but you were ages in Theatre and a girl has to sleep some time.'

She was keeping it light, as she had earlier, but although Jack acknowledged her arrival by opening his eyes, that was all the response she got.

Cal, who'd been standing at the foot of the bed with his arm around Gina, nodded tiredly at Kate, then led Gina away. Jill, who looked as if she hadn't slept for days, also departed, her shoulders slumped as if Jack's failure to respond was somehow her fault.

Kate continued to talk, while Charles sat beside her, watching the screen for any kind of response from his nephew.

Nothing—well, not nothing, but the changes were all negative. They were looking on while a healthy young man died for no apparent reason.

Hamish stood outside the room, watching through the window, seeing the urgency in Kate's pose as she bent over the bed, trying to force a reaction of any kind from Jack.

Apparently deciding there was nothing he could do, Charles left the room, wheeling to a stop beside Hamish so he, too, could watch through the window.

'I tried to phone his mother, but got an answering-machine. Philip thinks she might be skiing in New Zealand. Even if we ask the police over there to track the family down, it could be days before she gets here.'

The anguish in Charles's voice told Hamish far more than the words. The man was blaming himself for insisting the lad stayed here in Crocodile Creek.

'You did all you could,' Hamish assured him. 'His whole blood clotting time was within acceptable limits, we had the desmopressin on hand for Lucky, so you were able to infuse that into him before the op. They couldn't have done any more in a major city hospital, and shifting him again might have provoked this problem earlier.'

But Charles refused to be comforted.

'I shouldn't have assumed my way was the best way,' he said bitterly. 'Damn it all, Hamish. There's far too much bad blood in this family already, without me having more of it on my hands.'

'You've already done what you can to get Jim and Honey

Cooper back on their feet and to end the feud between the Coopers and the Wetherbys,' he reminded Charles.

'Sure!' Charles growled. 'I patch things up just fine then let the father of their grandchild die. It'll start all over again!'

'Not if Kate has any say in it,' Hamish said, nodding to where Kate was ordering the young man to live.

Standing helplessly beside the bed, her gaze snapping from Jack to the monitor and back again, Kate thought about the story Hamish had told her. A family feud that had torn this modern-day Romeo from his Juliet.

His Juliet! His girlfriend! The baby! She swung around to see Hamish talking to Charles outside the window.

Leaving Jack's side, she headed out the door.

'Megan? Where's Megan? Is she still in the hospital? Or in town? Can we get her here? She's the one person to whom he might respond.'

Hamish, who'd heard Jack's insistence that Megan was the only girl for him, caught on fastest.

'She's living at Christina's house. I'll go there now.'

But Charles held him back.

'You think he cares about her? According to Jim, he hasn't seen her for six months.'

'He cares,' Hamish said, and Charles nodded.

'Then go and get her. I'll handle Jim.'

Satisfied she'd done what she could, Kate returned to Jack's side, and continued urging a response from him, but through the window she saw Charles wheel away—to tell Jim Cooper his daughter's boyfriend was now in the hospital?

Would Megan come? Kate was frustrated that she didn't know more about the dynamics of the relationship between Megan and Jack. There was a baby—but did Megan care about its father?

The question was answered very soon afterwards when a

plump young woman came racing into the ICU, Hamish hurrying rather ineffectually behind her.

'Where is he? Where's Jack?' she demanded.

Emily came out from behind the monitor to intercept her.

'Hush, Megan,' she said quietly. 'Calm down, love. You're not long out of here yourself.'

But Megan was beyond stopping. With one swift glance around the sterile space, she found which room held the man she sought and, stepping around Emily, headed straight for it.

But was it love or anger driving her? Kate had no idea, but she wasn't going to take any chances. She intercepted Megan as the excited young woman burst through the door.

'He's very sick. Don't shock him,' she warned, then put her arms around the newcomer as Megan's face crumpled and she let out an anguished cry.

'I wouldn't hurt him,' she whispered. 'I love him!'

The plaintive declaration speared pain deep into Kate's heart, but she held her ground, talking quietly to Megan to calm her before she approached Jack's bed.

'Hamish said there was no reason for him to be so sick,' Megan whimpered, allowing Kate to hold her while she stared at the pale, depleted figure on the bed.

'No, it just seems as if he's given up.'

'He can't do that. He's got a baby,' Megan protested. 'He can't die without knowing about Jackson.'

'He won't die,' Kate promised—both fiercely and foolishly—then she led Megan close to the bed, took Jack's hand and spoke to him again.

'Hey, Jack, I've got a surprise for you. This will make you open your eyes.'

She put his hand into Megan's and stepped back, while Megan collapsed into the chair beside the bed and brushed her lips across his hand. Tears spilled onto his skin and dampened the sheets, and Kate backed up against the wall and waited, knowing Megan needed to get her own emotions under control before she could speak to Jack.

'Jack, I'm here, and I love you so much. Please, don't leave me again. I tried so hard to believe I didn't love you. I even told myself I could live without you, but seeing you again I know I can't, so don't leave me, Jack, don't leave me again.'

Megan used his hand to wipe away fresh tears, and Kate found herself swallowing hard and hoping her eyes weren't brimming too obviously.

'I need you, Jack,' Megan continued, her voice steady although she was trembling all over. 'You have no idea how much I need you—especially now.'

She glanced up at Kate, despairing questions in her eyes. Was she talking too much? Was it doing any good?

And the big one—should she tell him about the baby?

Or maybe Kate imagined that one. She hoped so because she had no idea how a young man might respond to the unexpected news he was a father.

'Keep talking, that's all you can do,' she said.

Megan obeyed, telling Jack she'd been here in hospital herself and though she'd been sick she'd kept thinking of him and that had kept her going.

'We need each other, Jack,' she said, imploring a response from him. 'We're meant to be together.'

But Kate, who was watching the monitor all the time, willing a change in the slowly declining peaks, knew the words were being lost somewhere in the caverns of emptiness inside the young man.

Megan gave her one last despairing look, then threw the last dice.

'We have a baby, Jack. A little boy. I called him Jackson—you know, Jack's son. He's been sick too, Jack, he has a bad heart, but he's a fighter, our baby, a real little champ.'

There! The spike Kate had been praying for happened, and

she turned her attention from the monitor to the patient. Jack had opened his eyes, startling Megan so much she began to cry again.

'A baby?' Kate lip-read the question, as his voice was strangled by the tubes in his nose and mouth.

Megan held both his hands now, and nodded, tears falling all over him.

'A baby called Jackson. I'll bring him in to show you just as soon as you're well enough.'

'Now!'

Neither Megan nor Kate could decipher the word, until Jack repeated it.

Megan turned to Kate.

'The baby's still here in the nursery because he ran a temperature last week and he's still not feeding well. Can I bring him now?'

Kate had no idea of the protocol of tiny babies in this ICU, but Charles had obviously heard the conversation, for he was at the door.

'I'll get Lucky for you,' he said to Megan, then he smiled apologetically and added, 'Jackson! I must remember Jackson!'

He wheeled away, Megan returning to Jack's side to tell him the baby was on the way, and that he looked just like his father, and now Jack was back they could be a family.

And although Jack's eyes had closed, Kate could tell he hadn't slipped away from them again. He'd left that no-man's land between life and death and, hopefully, wouldn't return there for a long, long time.

Leaving the little family in the ICU in Charles's hands, Kate returned to the house, but now, in daylight, she knew she wouldn't sleep. Not that there was time for sleep. It was after six and she'd been told the hospital car left for Wygera at eight. She changed into her running gear, slipped on her trainers and once again went quietly out of the house.

This time, however, she heard noises in the old building, voices from the side veranda—CJ and Cal, she guessed, while Mike was sitting at the kitchen table, talking into a mobile phone.

He lifted a hand in salute to Kate, then jotted something in a small notebook on the table in front of him.

Kate waved back and continued on her way. A good run over the headland would shake away the cobwebs her interrupted night's sleep had left behind, and prepare her for whatever lay ahead.

She began slowly, pacing herself as she crossed the dewy grass, relishing the salt tang of the air as she drew it deeply into her lungs. Then her rhythm picked up and she extended her pace so she reached the sun-drenched summit winded enough to need to bend over to regain her breath.

So it wasn't until she straightened that the full beauty of the place struck her—the blue-green of the sea, the curved hump of an island on the horizon, the golden sands curling around the cove.

Finally, a house by the sea. Maybe she'd extend her contract. Maybe if her father wanted her…

Best not to think about it, she reminded herself, but the warning came too late. Thinking about the father she didn't know had disrupted the blissful serenity her run had given her, and now, as she stared out at the peaceful sea, disquiet was growing again within her.

Or was the disquiet because she sensed she was no longer alone on the bluff?

She turned, wondering if it was one of the housemates she hadn't yet met who was joining her in her silent communion with the sea.

It *was* a housemate, but one she knew—one she'd been trying not to think about as she'd run across the tough, springy grass of the headland.

'Kate.'

Hamish was close enough to shield her from the breeze that had been fidgeting at her clothing, and her name was both an acknowledgement and a greeting.

She nodded in reply then decided to walk along the clifftop, assuming, if he wanted her company, he'd fall in beside her.

But instead he grasped her elbow, effectively halting her progress and, at the same time, turning her towards him.

He stared at her for a moment, as if uncertain who she was.

'This is the most ridiculous situation,' he grumbled at her.

'Walking on a clifftop?'

'No!'

The grumble had become a growl.

'Then what?'

Batman would never have asked that question.

Batman would have known the answer without having to ask.

In actual fact, Kate knew the answer, too, because she could feel the attraction between them simmering in the clean morning air.

Pollution, that was what it was...

And, as Hamish had said, it was a ridiculous situation. They'd barely met. He was going away.

'Do you know how badly I want to kiss you?' His voice was tight enough to make the words sound clipped and harsh.

'I can guess,' Kate admitted, as her own body hummed with a quite absurd desire to do the same to him. 'But I'm sure it's just proximity that's doing this to us. We shared a night of tension, out there in the gorge with Jack, and it drew us closer together than a month of normal company might do.'

Did she sound down to earth and together, or had her internal flutters botched the job?

'Do you honestly believe a work-related bond would make me want to kiss you? I've worked with Cal for two years and never wanted to kiss him. Or Emily. Or Christina.'

Hamish didn't seem to be moving but his body was narrowing the gap between the two of them so now she could feel its warmth.

'I should hope not,' Kate retorted, edging backwards because the warmth was dangerous. 'You can't go around kissing all your colleagues. And that includes me. Apart from anything else, with me, anyway, it's impractical. Think about it, Hamish! Starting something would be idiotic. You're going home in less than three weeks and I'm here on a mission. It's a perfect example of the wrong time and the wrong place.'

She was trying hard not to look directly at him—looking at Hamish being something more safely done from a distance—but she knew for sure he'd greeted this prime example of common sense with a frown.

Knew for sure he'd closed the gap between them once again!

'Wrong time? Wrong place? Is there such a thing with kisses?' he demanded, then, without waiting for her answer, his lips closed on hers, warm and firm and all-encompassing, claiming her mouth like a trophy, tempting her lips open with an inciting tongue, luring from her a response she knew she shouldn't give.

The kiss lasted until her knees gave out and she slumped against his body.

'Hamish!'

The word she'd intended as a protest came out more like an endearment, encouraging him to lock his arms around her body and draw her close against him, supporting her, so he could continue to plunder her mouth at will.

The sweet invasion warmed the lonely places in her heart, seducing her with its promise, and although her head knew kissing Hamish was not at all a good idea, her heart longed for more—her body demanded more.

No! Kate broke away, frightened by the intensity of whatever it was between them.

'I'm going back,' she said abruptly, and ran away, heading

down towards the house—hoping she might find her lost sanity along the way.

CJ was on the top step again, but as Kate drew close Cal appeared, hoisting the child onto his shoulders and carrying him down the steps.

'I'm taking a spaceship to child care,' CJ told her, waving a cardboard contraption in the air above Cal's head. 'And Mr Grubb's taken Rudolph to get his shots so he won't follow me today.'

Kate congratulated them both on the excellent spaceship, wished CJ a happy day then took the steps two at a time, crossing the veranda and finding Emily in the kitchen with Mike.

'Hi, Kate. Have you met Mike? Our second chopper pilot and paramedic.'

Emily had a possessive hand resting on Mike's shoulder, and the same sheen in her eyes that Kate had noticed in Gina's the previous day.

The love epidemic?

'We met last night,' Kate explained. 'Jack OK?'

Emily beamed at her.

'More OK than he was earlier. We'd thought of bringing Megan in, but we had no idea if he'd want to see her or not. He hadn't been in touch with her for six months, so we thought maybe he'd be more upset than he already was.'

She paused for breath, then added, 'Hamish said Jack told you both how he felt about his girlfriend, and how he'd tried to go and visit her.'

'It's often a case of whatever works in medicine, isn't it?' Mike said, patting Emily's hand, which still rested on his shoulder. 'How was your run?'

The change of subject was somewhat abrupt and Mike's question was innocent enough, yet Kate felt colour surge into her cheeks. Could people see the headland from the kitchen? Or had Mike been outside and seen her kissing Hamish?

'It was fine,' she said, 'but I'm very sweaty. I've got to change for work.'

And with that she escaped to her room.

It didn't matter who saw what, she told herself, but she knew it did. After the public humiliation she'd endured with Daniel and Lindy, Kate was determined her private life would be just that—private.

Not that she intended having a private life with Hamish.

She'd have a shower, grab a bowl of cereal—she would have to find out about cooking and shopping rosters—then go over to the hospital well in time for the trip to Wygera.

If she was early enough, she could get her roster from Jill. Maybe she could get the doctors' rosters as well. Then all she had to do was make sure she was always busy if she and Hamish happened to have corresponding time off.

Avoidance—that was the answer.

The white station wagon with the 24-hour-rescue emblem she was beginning to recognise as belonging to the hospital, pulled up in front of her, the driver—from his sheer size—unmistakable.

'Charles or Cal usually do Wygera clinics,' Hamish said cheerfully, reaching across to open the door for her, 'but Cal's got a theatre list today and Charles wants to stay close to Jack, so you're stuck with me again.'

Kate eyed him with suspicion. It wasn't so much that he might have engineered this togetherness—after all, he didn't know about her avoidance decision—but the way he was acting so…well, colleaguey!

Weird!

Uncomfortable, even.

But two could play at pretending they hadn't exchanged heated kisses on a headland a bare hour earlier.

'Will you be helping me judge the swimming pool designs?'

'Oh, no, not me! That's your job, Sister Winship. Yours

alone, although remind me when we get there, I've got young Shane's model in the back of the car. He came in a few days ago with a burst appendix and as he had to finish his model in hospital we gave him an extra couple of days to get his entry in.'

Kate remembered the talk about the competition she'd heard the previous evening. And CJ's words as well.

'And CJ and Max's entry? They were working on it last night. Have you got that on board?'

Hamish turned and smiled at her, and she forgot swimming pools, and models, and a small boy who needed a cowboy hat.

This could *not* be happening!

'Cal has already ordered a cowboy hat for Max and he and CJ will get it as a consolation prize,' Hamish said. 'That was arranged after Rudolph ate the dressing sheds which they'd made out of dog biscuits.'

Kate had to laugh, but Hamish's tone made her feel uncomfortable.

He was either far, far better at this colleague stuff than she was, or his words about needing to kiss her had been just that—words.

Or maybe he tested women with a kiss.

Maybe he'd tested her and she'd failed.

The thought made her so depressed she remembered she was going to Wygera so she could see something of the countryside, and she looked out the window at the canefields through which they were passing, seeing nothing but a green blur, while her mind wondered just what the man beside her might have expected from a kiss.

Kissing ineptitude—was that why Daniel had chosen Lindy?

'Aboriginal community.'

Kate tuned back in to Hamish's conversation but it was too late. Not a word of it could she recall.

'I'm sorry, I missed that,' she said, facing him again, although that was dangerous when he might smile at any time.

'Canefields *are* fascinating,' he said, eyes twinkling to let her know he knew she hadn't seen them.

He knew too damn much!

'I was saying that as well as a swimming pool, Wygera needs some kind of industry. Perhaps industry is the wrong word, but a number of aboriginal communities like it are self-supporting. They run cattle stations, or tourist resorts. In the Northern Territory there are artists' colonies. The problem is Wygera's close enough to Croc Creek for some of the men to be employed there, but there's not enough employment in town for all of them. Nor does everyone want to drive fifty miles back and forth to work.'

'So kids grow up and leave home,' Kate said, understanding the problem of the lack of employment in small towns.

'Or don't leave home and get into trouble,' Hamish said, sounding more gloomy than she'd ever heard him.

'You sound as if you really care,' she said, thinking how different he was from some city doctors she had known who felt their responsibilities ended when a patient walked out the door.

'Of course I care!' he snapped. 'I've worked with these people for two years and become friends with a number of them. Just because I'm going home, it doesn't mean I'll stop thinking about them. But until something happens to change things at Wygera, these clinic runs—well, doctors and nurses will go on treating symptoms rather than the problem.'

They'd turned off the main highway onto a narrower road which ran as straight as a ruler towards a high water tower.

'Wygera!' Hamish said, nodding towards the tower, and gradually, beneath it, a cluster of houses became evident. Dilapidated houses for the most part, with dogs dozing in the dirt in the shade cast by gutted car bodies. Kate recognised the look—there were suburbs in Melbourne where car bodies were the equivalent of garden gnomes in front-yard decor.

Beyond the houses, the ground sloped down to where thickly grouped trees suggested a creek or a river.

But if the town had a creek or river, why would it need a swimming pool?

CHAPTER SIX

HAMISH PULLED UP in front of a small building with a table and three chairs set up outside and a group of people lounging around on logs, chairs, or small patches of grass.

'Medicine, Wygera-style,' he said to Kate. 'If the weather's good we work outside, although there are perfectly adequate examination, waiting and treatment rooms inside the building.'

He nodded towards a stand of eucalypts some distance away, where more people lay around in the shade.

'They're your lot. We come out a couple of times a week, and today's well-baby day, but if you see anything that worries you, shoot the person over to me. Eye problems are the main worries with the kids, diabetes with the mums. They'll all have their cards with them—the health worker sees them before we arrive.'

Kate accepted all this information and advice, then, as a young man opened her door with a flourish, she stepped out and looked around her.

The place was nestled in the foothills of the mountains that divided the coastal plain from the cattle country further inland. The ground was bare and rocky, with grass struggling to grow here and there, mainly in the patches of shade.

'Your bag, ma'am,' Hamish said, handing her a square suitcase from the back of the station wagon. 'Scales, swabs, dressings and so on all inside, but Jake here will act as your runner if you need anything else.'

Kate took the bag, but the young man—presumably Jake—who had opened the car door lifted it out of her hand and led her towards the trees, where the shapes became women and children as Kate drew closer. Another table was set out there, with two chairs beside it, but Kate wondered if she might be better sitting on the grass with the women.

'Sit on the chair, then the women can put babies on your knee,' Jake told her, while another woman who Jake introduced as Millie got up from the grass and took the second chair.

'I'm the health worker here,' she said, unpacking the case and setting up the baby scales. 'I do the weighing.'

'Thanks,' Kate said, but she glanced towards the clinic building. Strange it didn't have its own scales.

'People take them to weigh fish and potatoes and bananas, not so good afterwards for babies,' Millie said, while Kate wondered if people in North Queensland had a special ability to read minds or if she'd always been so easy to read.

Though Hamish was a Scot, not a North Queenslander.

She almost glanced towards him, but remembered Millie and caught herself just in time.

'I'm Kate,' she said to the assembled throng, then she took her chair. 'Now, who's first?'

Some of the women giggled, and there was general shuffling, but Millie called a name and a pretty girl in blue jeans and a short tight top came forward, a tiny baby in her arms.

Kate looked at the girl's flat stomach, complete with navel ring, and decided she couldn't possibly have had a child, but Angela was indeed baby Joseph's mother.

'He just needs weighing and I'm worried about this rash,' she said, putting the baby on the table and whipping off his disposable nappy. 'See!'

The angry red rash in his groin and across his buttocks would have been hard to miss.

Kate delved into the bag, assuming she'd find a specimen tube and swab. Yes, it was as well equipped for a well-baby clinic as the equipment pack had been for Jack's retrieval. She wiped a swab across the rash, dropped it into the tube, and screwed the lid shut and completed the label, taking Joseph's full name from the card.

'Nappy rash, I told her,' Millie said. 'Said to leave off his nappies or use cloth ones on him.'

'I did leave his nappy off,' Angela protested, 'and it didn't get better, and I tried cloth nappies.'

'Actually, the latest tests seem to find that disposable nappies are less irritating to the skin than cloth ones,' Kate said gently, not wanting to put Millie off side, but wanting to get the message across to Angela. 'Also, if we look at the shiny surface of the rash and the way there are separate spots of it here and there, I think it might be candida—a yeast infection.'

'Like women get?' Angela asked, and Kate nodded.

'A similar thing. It's caused by yeast from the bowel and by bacteria and is more uncomfortable for poor Joseph than simple nappy rash, but there's a cream you can use that should clear it up.'

What next? From what she'd seen of the town, it didn't have a chemist's shop, so getting Hamish to write a prescription seemed pointless.

'Cream in the bag,' Millie said to Kate. Millie obviously knew far more about clinic visits than Kate did! 'This stuff stains his nappies so don't you be worrying about it,' Millie continued, addressing Angela this time, while Kate found the cream, one per cent hydrocortisone and three per cent iodochlorhydroxyquin—and, yes, the tube said it could leave a yellow stain.

Millie certainly knew more than Kate did!

'Spread it thinly over the sore part twice a day,' Kate told Angela. 'Like this.'

She used a treated cloth to wipe the little fellow's nether regions clean and another cloth to dry him off, then smeared a little of the cream over the bright scarlet rash. 'You really need just a thin smear—putting it on more thickly doesn't make the slightest difference. If it hasn't shown signs of improvement, come back…'

There wouldn't be a well-baby clinic more than once a fortnight but Kate remembered Hamish saying they did clinics, plural, each week.

'Come back and see whoever comes later in the week,' she finished, while Angela handed the baby and his card over to Millie for weighing and recording.

'You give Joseph to his gran and get back to school,' Millie told Angela when Joseph had his nappy on again and was ready to go.

'She's still at school?' Kate asked Millie, while they waited for the next patient.

'Last year, university next year. Wants to be a doctor. She'll do it, too. Her mother'll go to Townsville with her to mind Joseph while she studies. Girl's got guts and brains—just stupid in the heart.'

Stupid in the heart! It was such an apt phrase it stayed with Kate as she examined another eight babies and listened to the problems their mothers had. She brought some up to date on their triple antigens, administered Neosporin drops into weeping eyes, gave advice to mothers on weaning, solids, diarrhoea and contraception, Millie letting her know in unsubtle ways whether she agreed or disagreed with the advice dispensed.

'Lunch and judging time.'

Kate looked around to see Hamish approaching.

Stupid in the heart, Kate reminded herself just in case the reaction inside her had been something other than hunger manifesting itself.

'Why doesn't Millie take the well-baby clinic?' she asked Hamish as they drove further into the town. 'She knows the people and certainly knows as much if not more than I do.'

'She says the people take more notice of someone from the hospital. They go to Millie in between our visits then come to see us to confirm what she's told them.'

'And that doesn't drive her wild? That they don't believe her in the first place?'

Hamish smiled.

'I think it would take a lot to drive Millie wild. She just accepts that's the way things are and gets on with her job.'

And that's a salutary lesson for you, Kate told herself, then she gazed in astonishment at the building in front of her.

'What *is* this place?'

'Local hall. Funded by the federal government and designed in Canberra, which is why the roof is steeply pitched—so snow can slide off it.'

Kate was laughing as she got out of the car into the searing heat of what in North Queensland was considered cool spring weather, but once inside her laughter stopped, though a smile lingered on her lips.

The models, dozens of them, were set out on tables in the middle of the hall.

'So many? Boy, the people here are really enthusiastic about having a swimming pool.'

'You'd better believe it! But we'll eat first. Wygera does the best lunches of all our clinic runs,' Hamish said, leading her past the tables of exhibits to the back of the hall, where three women waited in a large kitchen.

'Cold roast beef and salad. That all right?' asked an older woman Hamish introduced as Mary.

'Sounds great,' Kate said, though she felt uncomfortable sitting at the table with Hamish while the women served and fussed over them, offering bread and butter to go with the salad, tea or coffee, then finally producing a luscious-looking trifle, decorated with chocolate curls.

'I bet the female staff refuse to do more than one Wygera trip a week,' Kate said, smiling at the women. 'I'd be the size of a house if I came here more often.'

'We like visitors, so why not show them how we feel with good food?' Mary said, then she cleared the table while one of the other women walked back into the hall with Kate.

'All the plans and models have numbers and the doctors who were here on Sunday, they have a list of the number and the names, so all you have to do is choose one and tell them the number. Dr Cal, he has the list.'

Kate turned around, thinking she might co-opt Hamish into helping her, but he was still in the kitchen, talking to Mary.

So she pulled her little notebook and pen out of her pocket and did an initial survey of the entries.

Round and round she went, slowly eliminating designs, until finally one was left. It had bits of dying bushes where trees would be planted, and tiny plastic animals sliding down plastic rulers to show waterslides. Scraps of drinking straws indicated where water would stream out from spa jets and what looked suspiciously like a hospital kidney dish represented the main pool.

'This is it,' she said to Hamish, who, with the other women, had now joined her in the hall and were eagerly awaiting the decision.

'But that's Shane's,' Hamish said, apparently recognising the model he'd brought into the hall earlier.

'Does that disqualify it in some way?' Kate asked.

'No, no, of course not,' Hamish said quickly, then he smiled. 'In fact, I think it's great. Poor kid's been sick as a dog since his appendix op, and this will cheer him right up.'

He turned to the three women.

'Will you keep it quiet or should we announce it straight away?'

'People will know straight away whether you tell or not,' Mary said. 'People always know things.'

This was no more relevant to her situation than the 'stupid hearts' comment had been, Kate told herself, yet 'people know things' joined the 'stupid in the heart' phrase in her head, as if both were philosophical concepts of prime importance in her life.

You do not *know* you're attracted to Hamish—you just think you could be, she reminded herself. But the phrase refused to budge.

'This afternoon we work together, usually doing a bit of minor surgery in the clinic itself. Some days there's a long list and other times we get an early mark.'

Hamish explained this as he carried Shane's model out to the station wagon. They would take it back to Crocodile Creek and pass it on to the architect, hoping he would at least follow the concept of this winning design.

Still in colleague mode, Kate registered, which was good— at least one of them would be totally focussed on work!

But Kate's mind found focus soon enough. Their first patient was a middle-aged man, Pete, with a fish hook caught in his wrist. As he peeled off a grubby bandage, Kate could see the angry red line that indicated infection running up his arm from the wound.

'You did the right thing, cutting off the barbed end and trying to pull it back through,' Hamish said, as he injected a local anaesthetic around the injured part. 'But slashing at yourself with razor blades to try to cut it out wasn't the brightest follow-up treatment.'

'M'mate did that,' Pete told them. 'We were up the river in the boat, and we'd had a few tinnies, and he thought he'd get it out.'

Now the wound was cleaned, Kate could see the slashes across the man's wrist, making it look like a particularly inept suicide attempt.

Or was it, and the fish hook just an excuse?

She glanced at Hamish, who was now probing the wounds carefully and competently, talking quietly to Pete about fish and fishing.

He was obviously a doctor who saw his patient as a person first while his easy camaraderie with the women at lunchtime had suggested they saw him as a friend.

'Ah, I can see it now. Forceps, Kate.'

Recalled to duty, Kate passed the implement but, try as he might, Hamish couldn't pull the hook free.

'I'll have to cut down to it,' he said, and Kate produced a packaged scalpel for him, carefully peeling off the protective covering and passing it to him.

'Soluble sutures for inside and some tough thread for the skin—these guys don't treat their wounds with any consideration,' Hamish told her, as he cut into the man's wrist. 'And check Pete's card for his tetanus status.'

Kate found the sutures Hamish would need, prepared a tetanus injection and another of penicillin, certain Pete would need an antibiotic boost even if Hamish gave him tablets. Another check of his card showed he'd had penicillin before so they had no need to worry about allergies.

But it was the need for his last dose of penicillin that drew Kate's attention. A fish hook in his foot?

'Was Pete plain unlucky or are fish hooks particularly aggressive up here in North Queensland?' she asked Hamish as, three hours later, they drove away from Wygera. 'He had one in his foot only six months ago.'

Hamish turned to smile at her.

'Pete's mad keen on fishing. He took me out once, but once was enough. I know the boat we were in was bigger than the crocodiles I kept seeing lazing on the bank, but not by much. In fact, it got flimsier and flimsier the longer we stayed out, especially when some of the crocs got off the bank and started swimming towards us.'

'Real crocodiles?'

Kate knew it had been a stupid question as soon as she'd asked it, but she'd just blurted the words out.

'Too, too real,' Hamish said, 'although before that day I thought Crocodile Creek was just a name. You know, like Snake Gully. Maybe someone once saw a snake there, but it doesn't mean there are dozens of the things in the gully.'

'But there are dozens of crocodiles in the creek?'

Kate looked nervously out the car window. How far from creeks did crocodiles travel? And hadn't she heard they could run faster than a horse?

Could a horse run faster than a car?

'Hey, we're safe,' Hamish said gently, slowing the car and resting his hand on her shoulder.

'I know that!' Kate snapped. Now she compared the two experiences, thinking of crocodiles in a creek not far from where she'd sat and looked at babies was freaking her out far more than the man with the gun had.

Then she'd been able to snuggle close to Hamish for protection. Now she'd look stupid if she straddled the gear lever to get close to him, which, from other points of view, would not be a good idea anyway.

'I can see why they need a swimming pool. I wouldn't want to swim in a creek with crocodiles.'

Somehow talk of swimming pools and crocodiles kept them going for most of the journey, though tension built inside Kate until she wondered if she'd burst with it.

But when Hamish pulled off the road into a parking area that gave a view over the town and the cove and the sea beyond it, she guessed she wasn't the only one feeling the crackling in the air between them. He was just better at hiding it.

He turned towards her, his eyes looking black in the shadowy car.

'Is it the wrong time and the wrong place, Kate?'

He kissed her gently, but even a gentle kiss fired her heartbeats.

'Can you deny there's something special between us? Can you deny you feel what I feel when we're together—deny there's magic in our kisses?'

Kate tried, she really did, but she couldn't, and in the end she had to shake her head.

'But it's not about magic, Hamish, it's about trust.'

He kissed her again.

'I know that, which is why we don't need to hurry things—don't need to put the pressure of a three-week time limit on getting to know each other. I know you want to find your father, but there's every chance, particularly if we involve people from the hospital, you can do that in a few days. Then why don't you come to Scotland with me? No pressure or promises. Just come, to see how things might work out.'

The strength of his hands, and the warmth they generated, seeped deep into Kate's body, but it was all too soon, and taking warmth from someone else was far too dangerous.

'I don't think so, Hamish,' she said quietly, and sat back in her seat.

At least now crocodiles weren't the main worry in her mind.

Hamish paused for a few seconds, then reversed out of their parking space and pulled out onto the highway, starting up a conversation about the necessity to watch out for kangaroos on the roads around dawn and dusk.

It was, she was learning, typical of this kind, caring, empathetic man—not play-acting at being a colleague but genuinely trying to set her at ease.

She was beginning to admire Colleague Hamish.

Back at the hospital, they unpacked the car then, as Hamish went to report to Charles, she walked through to the ICU to visit Jack.

* * *

Jack was lying with his eyes closed, and though he opened them when Kate said hello, his eyelids soon drooped, but the smile on his face, even as he slept, told Kate all she needed to know.

She dropped into the chair beside Megan, who was anchored to the bed by Jack's hand clasping both of hers.

'Are you OK?'

Megan nodded, a tremulous smile on her lips.

'Dad came to see him,' she whispered to Kate, 'before they transferred him to Townsville for his bypass. He told Jack he'd better hurry and get better, because he was needed out at Cooper's Crossing.'

Megan's smile improved as she added proudly, 'That's our place. Dad wants him there, but not right away. Dad and Charles have been talking. They think Jack and I should get agriculture training—they say we should spend a few years at university so we're sure we know what we're doing. Charles says there's enough money to fund it and that there's child care at university.'

She paused and her smile, if possible, grew even more radiant.

'University, Kate! Can you imagine? Then we'll come home and with water we'll make Cooper's Crossing viable again. It'll be as good as Wetherby, good enough to support two families— the Ransomes and the Coopers. Together.'

As Megan's expression suggested this was the most wonderful of ideas, Kate gave her a hug and told her how happy she was, hiding her own reservations about this happy-ever-after-ending until she'd left the ICU.

Charles and Hamish were talking outside the ED and though she didn't want to interrupt—and certainly didn't want to get entangled with Hamish again, as colleague or kisser—she did want to know if Harry was proceeding with his enquiries.

She hesitated, and Charles saw her and settled her indecision.

'We were just talking about you,' he called to her.

'Surely I haven't been here long enough to be in trouble,' she said lightly, smiling at Charles.

'Far from it,' Charles assured her. 'No, we were talking about Jack. Harry really needs to see him and, for Jack's sake, the sooner the mess with his mates Todd and Digger is sorted out, the better. Emily says, providing there's no setback, we can move him out of ICU tomorrow, and once he's on a ward it will be hard to keep Harry away from him.'

'You'll stay with him when Harry interviews him?' Kate asked anxiously.

Charles looked at a point somewhere over her head.

'That's actually why we were talking about you. I know you were employed to work the ED here, but I wondered if you'd mind working the men's ward for the next few days. I don't want to seem as if I'm standing guard over the lad, it will make him look bad, but I'd like to think he has someone he knows and trusts hovering around. I'll tell Harry he's still sufficiently ill that I want a nurse with him while he's interviewed. Would you do it?'

'Of course,' Kate said. 'Do I see Jill? She'll need to change someone else's shift as well as mine.'

'I'll fix it up with Jill. What were you working tomorrow?'

'Early shift,' Kate told him. 'Six to three.'

Charles smiled at her.

'Well, isn't this your lucky day? We'll transfer Jack in the morning, and he'll need to rest after the move, so I won't let Harry near him until the afternoon. If you could do the afternoon shift, midday to nine, that should cover the time Harry's likely to be there, and if you're already on the ward, it won't look as if we've brought in someone especially to be with Jack.'

Kate smiled at Charles's obvious satisfaction with this plan. In fact, it pleased her as well. She'd have the morning free to explore the town and, once she'd found out how shopping and cooking rosters worked in the house, maybe shop as well.

She nodded to the two men and walked away, her thoughts veering between Hamish, who'd been silent throughout her talk to Charles, and Jack—was he well enough for Harry to question him?

'Are you happy taking on the role of protector?' Hamish fell in beside her. 'Do you feel you'd be able to stop Harry's questioning if you felt it necessary?'

Kate stopped and turned towards him.

'Medical question?' she asked, feeling warmth within, although he wasn't touching her.

'Medical question,' he confirmed, though the look in his eyes suggested he was feeling things not entirely medical.

'You bet your life I'd stop the questioning if I felt it was affecting his recovery in any way.'

'Mama bear protecting her cub?' Hamish teased, and Kate had to agree.

'I'm probably the very worst person to have there, because I do feel over-protective about Jack, but the slightest sign he might be tiring and Harry will be out of there.'

Hamish smiled at her.

'Word gets around the hospital quickly. When I hear Harry's arrived I might drop by, in case you need moral support.'

'And you're not over-protective?'

Hamish shrugged in a way that suggested agreement, leaving Kate to wonder if it was Jack or her that Hamish was protecting.

They walked out into the scented garden that drew Kate like a magnet, together only as colleagues, she was sure.

Its potent spell filled her head with pleasure, so worries over Kissing Hamish and Colleague Hamish were banished to the far reaches of her brain, and even her concern for Jack lost its hard, knobbly edges of doubt and dread.

CHAPTER SEVEN

HARRY FAILED TO arrive the next day, and Jill explained she'd like Kate to stay on the ward until he did come. Not a bad idea, as far as Kate was concerned, as she hadn't seen Hamish all day, whereas in the ED, if a child came in, she'd have had to call him as he was the doctor with the most paediatric experience in the hospital.

And being on duty until nine meant she could eat dinner at the hospital, and by the time she'd signed off and walked back to the house, it was late enough to go straight to bed, pleading tiredness should any of her housemates be hanging around.

The arrangement was perfect as far as Hamish-avoidance went.

Until she had to walk through the kitchen on her way to her room! He was over by the bench, waiting for the electric kettle to boil.

'Cup of tea?'

She checked her watch and studied him suspiciously.

'Were you waiting for me to come off duty?'

'Me?'

All innocence!

But then he smiled. 'Of course I was. I haven't seen you all day. Do you think I'd miss this opportunity? Now, did you say yes to tea?'

'No, I didn't,' Kate said crossly, although her mouth had

suddenly gone dry and she could kill for a cup of tea. 'And not seeing each other is a good idea, Hamish. I don't want to get into another relationship—not now, not here, not anywhere.'

He had turned his back, busying himself with cups and the kettle, and finally turned back and set a cup of tea on the table in front of her.

'You'd deny the magic?'

He spoke so softly she barely heard him. She wanted to yell, to tell him she'd had magic before and it had let her down, but she knew that what she and Daniel had shared had been an illusion—a magic trick, not the real thing at all. Only it had taken her longer than it had Daniel to work that out.

She picked up the cup of tea and sipped at it, eyeing Hamish cautiously over the rim.

'I'm not answering that, and I'm taking my tea through to my room.'

Would he argue? Pursue her?

Not Hamish. She answered her own question even before she heard his quiet 'Goodnight, Kate.'

So with a cup of tea in her hand, and loneliness beyond measuring in her heart, she walked through to her bedroom.

Hamish watched her walk away then took himself out onto the back veranda, settling into the old settee.

He needed to get rid of the baggage of his feelings and think this through with cool, unemotional logic.

Was he stupid, pursuing this attraction Kate obviously didn't want?

Yes.

So he should stop.

Right.

Would he?

Didn't even need to ask that question. This was different. This was special. This was something he'd never felt before…

* * *

Jack's condition improved steadily, and the following afternoon he watched Megan feed the baby, then held his son for a short time, before nodding off to sleep.

Megan was in the nursery, bathing Jackson before returning him to his crib, and Kate was putting a new dressing on Jack's wound when Harry wandered in.

'OK if we talk a bit?' he said to Jack, while Kate tried to act as if she was part of the furniture.

Jack did his eye-closing thing, but Kate knew he was refreshed and this was probably a good time for Harry to question him.

'You have to talk to Harry some time,' she said quietly. 'Why not at least start now. I'll be here, and if I see you getting tired I'll send Harry away, but at least start, Jack.'

He opened his eyes, looked at her for a moment, then nodded and turned to Harry.

'I honestly had no idea that they were anything more than cattle drovers,' he said. 'Not at first.'

'And who were "they"?'

Jack looked startled.

'Todd and Digger of course.'

'That's all the names you knew?'

Jack nodded.

'Met them in a pub out past Gunyamurra. They had a camp in an old station house way out on the edges of some property. Could even have been Wetherby Downs, but it was a place I'd never been. Todd said they had to hold these cattle there because they were expecting more.'

Kate had finished the dressing and now she took Jack's arm, unobtrusively holding his wrist so she could feel if his pulse began to race or falter.

Jack sipped from a glass of water, then continued.

'About the time of the Gunyamurra rodeo they gave me some time off—I tried to visit Megan but couldn't get the right lifts. I thought they were going to the rodeo because they kept talking about it, but when I got back they'd brought more cattle in. That's when I saw the brands.'

'What brands?' Harry asked, as Megan walked back into the ward and, seeing Harry with Jack, came flying across to the bed.

'It's OK, Megan,' Kate said quietly, but Megan was not to be stopped.

'He's still too sick!' she yelled at Harry. 'Can't you see that?' Then she turned her fury on Kate. 'You should have stopped him.'

Behind her, Kate sensed another presence and turned to see that Hamish had come in quietly.

'He has to answer questions some time, Megan,' Hamish told her, but Megan refused to be appeased, and as Jack had closed his eyes again, this time with a finality Kate recognised, she indicated to Harry to walk away. She followed him out of the room, leaving Hamish to reassure Megan that her loved one was all right.

'Jack *was* getting tired,' Kate said to Harry. 'Why don't you come back in the morning? Patients are always fresher then. And in the morning Megan is due to spend some time with Susie, learning massage techniques for Jackson.'

Harry smiled.

'She was as fierce as a mother bear protecting her cub, wasn't she?' he said, and Kate nodded, though she was thinking not of Megan's behaviour but of Hamish, who had said the same thing to her the previous evening.

Hamish who was now holding Megan in his arms and no doubt whispering all the soothing, special, comforting things she needed to hear.

He *was* special…

Get your mind off him and onto your patient! Think Jack!

Kate set her mind to it, recalling the questions and answers. Jack had been talking easily about the cattle until he'd come to the bit about the brands.

'Worries?'

So much for getting Hamish out of her mind by thinking about Jack! But, then, maybe Hamish could help.

Kate glanced back into the room to see Megan sitting quietly at Jack's side, while he apparently slept, and turned her attention to the man she'd been determined to avoid.

'Jack was upset by the questions before Megan came in,' she explained. 'Remember when you were telling me what might have happened and you said Jack might have recognised the Wetherby Downs brand and realised the cattle were stolen?'

'In the cave?'

Kate nodded.

'Well, what if they weren't Wetherby cattle but Cooper cattle he recognised? Would he want to admit that? When Jim had just welcomed him to the family and Megan was nearby to hear?'

Hamish put his hand on her shoulder.

'Do you always take on the worries of the world?'

'It's not the world, it's Jack,' she retorted. 'And if Harry comes back in the morning to cover this tricky stuff, I'd like to be there, but I'm not a lawyer and maybe that's what he needs.'

She used her own hand to lift his away and determinedly ignored the effects of both touches, but he wasn't going to be put off.

'It's your tea-break—I checked,' he said. 'Let's go talk to Charles about it.'

He led the way, guiding her along corridors and tapping quietly at the door before entering. Jill was there, which pleased Kate who was beginning to feel she was making a fuss about nothing but obscurely felt Jill might understand.

Jill could also change her shifts!

Charles greeted them as if he was used to small staff delegations wandering through his door, and asked how he could help.

'Kate will explain,' Hamish offered, so she brought Charles up to date and explained her worries.

'So,' she added, directly to Jill this time, 'I know it's a nuisance to keep switching shifts around, but if I could work maybe nine to six tomorrow, I'd be there in the morning when Harry comes, and still there in the afternoon if he happens to be held up.'

Jill assured her it would be OK but she was obviously as worried about Jack as Kate was.

'Is it time to bring in a lawyer for him?' Hamish asked Charles.

He thought about it for a minute, then shook his head.

'At the moment it's all pretty low key. Harry's getting the information he needs—there is an old homestead out on one of the back blocks of Wetherby, by the way, but no one's kept cattle on that block for years so Jack wouldn't have known of it. Anyway, Harry's happy and Jack's not too distressed, and the way I look at it, if he can prove he had time off when the cattle were stolen—'

'He hitched lifts to try to get to Megan,' Kate broke in. 'We only have to find the people who gave him lifts and we can prove he wasn't there.'

Charles smiled at her.

'We'll find them,' he promised, but, though he sounded confident, when Kate turned to close his office door behind her and Hamish as they left, she caught him frowning.

Had he only said it to make her feel better?

'Now tea?'

How could someone make such ordinary words seductive?

'No!'

The single word snapped out and hung in the air for so long she finally had to add a feeble 'Thank you' before she marched off back to the ward.

Didn't he know she was avoiding him?

Of course he didn't! She'd practically leapt at his suggestion that they talk to Charles together.

Harry arrived at ten the next morning, while Kate was hanging a new bag of fluid on Jack's drip stand.

'You getting preferential treatment here, Jack?' he asked. 'A pretty nurse all to yourself?'

'I've only just got to him,' Kate protested, knowing Jack would be embarrassed by the question. 'I didn't like to disturb him earlier when Megan was here, and Mr Roberts needed a bit of TLC.'

She checked the calibrations on the drip and picked up Jack's chart, knowing she had to look busy if she wanted to hang around.

'So, we were up to where your mates—'

'They weren't my mates!' Jack snapped, then, as Kate brushed his arm with her hand, he relented. 'Digger was OK.'

'Well,' Harry continued, 'we were up to where Todd and Digger took you back to the old homestead and there were more cattle there.'

Jack nodded.

'I saw the brands and asked if they'd bought the cattle from Jim Cooper—that's Megan's dad. I'd sometimes helped her, you see, mending the fences. It's how we met. Some of their cattle got in with ours and Philip went berserk, saying they were rubbish and he didn't want them polluting his stock, but although they were in poor condition, they were good cattle.'

Kate smiled to herself. Jack might have been a city kid like she had been, but he'd soon learnt.

'Anyway, I asked Todd if he'd bought them and he said yes, the place was going down the drain and Jim wanted rid of them—and I knew things were bad with the Coopers so it seemed OK. But then Todd and Digger started fooling around with the brands and that didn't seem right. So I left.'

'Did you tell them you were leaving?'

Jack shook his head.

'But I had to take the bike—Todd had two two-wheeler bikes and a four-wheeler he let me use. And taking the bike was stealing—so I left a note to say I'd leave it up near the highway, and as soon as I had some money I'd send him some for the inconvenience.'

'So he knew exactly which way you'd head?'

'I guess!'

Jack sounded more defeated than tired, but Kate felt he'd had enough, so she signalled to Harry that it was time to leave.

To her surprise, he didn't argue, and Kate wondered if he'd been as affected by Jack's patent honesty as she had been. Here was a kid from the city, helping his girlfriend mend fences on her property, worrying about her father's cattle, escaping from criminals, yet leaving a note to say which way he was going!

She smiled at the young man on the bed. Some might say it was stupidity rather than honesty, but she couldn't believe any jury in the world would find him guilty of whatever charges Harry might choose to lay against him.

In fact, if she could find out who had given him lifts and prove he hadn't been with the men when they'd stolen the cattle, Harry couldn't lay charges at all.

Another job for Batman and Robin?

Shaking her head at the intrusion of the stupid joke she'd come up with in the cave, she got on with her work. The whole idea of avoidance was that it got the other person out of the forefront of your mind.

Kate loved the walk from the hospital to the back of the house. There was a path, of course, from the front of the hospital to the front of the house, but that didn't go through the garden.

The Agnes Wetherby Memorial Garden, she'd discovered it was called. Planted in honour of Charles's grandmother—Jack's great-grandmother.

Jack was doing well—medically—and Harry hadn't reappeared to ask more questions in the afternoon, so Kate, Jack and Megan had all decided to take that as a good sign.

But apart from finding out who had given Jack a lift—and she had no idea how to go about that—she couldn't do much to help, so she wouldn't think of Jack's problems now. Although not thinking of Jack left a space in her mind, which was dangerous because spaces in her mind inevitably filled up with thoughts of Hamish.

The Hamish who had kissed her on the hill, not Colleague Hamish who had first appeared when he'd driven her to Wygera. Hamish kissing away her fear of crocodiles. Or had he been kissing away her fear of commitment? Hamish looking hurt when she'd refused to have tea with him yesterday.

It had been tea, for heavens' sake, and there'd have been a dozen people in the dining room, yet she'd seen the flare of disappointment in his eyes and had felt the touch of that flare in her heart.

'You're stupid in the heart,' she muttered to herself, and turned her attention to the garden.

Yesterday she'd discovered the source of a new perfume in the garden and she wanted to pick a stem of the pale pink pendulous flowers and ask someone to identify them for her. Actually, she'd pick the top of the stem—the whole stem, like the leaves that sheltered them, being taller than she was.

She had just succeeded in her task and was sniffing the rich, sweet scent when she heard the strumming of a guitar, but it wasn't until she reached the bottom of the steps she recognised the tune.

'K-K-K-Katie swallowed a ha'penny, a penn'orth of fish, a ha'porth of chips the day before—'

'The day before that,' Kate joined in, 'she swallowed the doormat, now she's trying to swallow the key of the kitchen door!'

She beamed up at Hamish, who was slumped in the old settee on the back veranda, his guitar across his lap.

'My grandad used to sing that to me. I always thought he'd made it up, but if you know it, too…'

Hamish saw the radiant smile fade from her face and read the cause of its disappearance with ease. Unexpected pain stabbed deep into his gut. Getting to know how this woman thought wasn't all beer and skittles.

And the fact that she was trying to keep him at arm's length wasn't doing one thing to curb his body's reaction every time he saw her. Rather the opposite, in fact.

'Come here!' he ordered, setting aside his guitar and standing up to enforce his order should it be necessary.

But Kate obeyed, coming wearily up the steps towards him, halting in front of him, summoning a shadow of her earlier smile and snapping a cheeky salute with a spray of flowers she'd been holding in her hand.

'Oh, Kateling!' he whispered softly, then he put his arm around her shoulders and led her to the settee.

It had been sat on so often by courting couples that it sagged conveniently in the middle, so any attempt to not sit close was met by defeat. This helped him tuck her small body close to his far larger one, the closest to a hug or cuddle Kate would allow.

'Just because he wasn't a blood relation, it doesn't mean he didn't love you with all of his heart.'

She turned and stared at him.

'How do you do it?' she demanded. 'How do you know what I'm thinking?'

He had to smile.

'Never play poker, kid!' If he kept it light he could tighten his arm and give her half a hug. Half a hug was friendship, not involvement. 'You've got the most expressive face I've ever seen.'

Kate sighed then, joy of joys, rested her head on his shoulder and gazed out over the placid waters of the cove.

'I know that in my head—about Grandad and my parents loving me,' she admitted sadly. 'It's in my heart I'm having trouble.'

Tell me about it! But Hamish kept his comment to himself. Having Kate this close was bliss, but one false move and she'd skitter away again, hiding behind the barricades of remembered pain.

'In my heart I've got this alone thing happening. I know it's stupid, but I can't seem to get around it. Anyway, smell this.'

She thrust her frond of flowers under his nose.

'Isn't it beautiful? Do you know what it is? Do you know why Charles doesn't like me?'

'Charles doesn't like you? You're asking me to identify a flower for you—it's ginger, by the way. I liked the scent so much myself I asked Jill about it. Then you switch to some cockamamie question about Charles not liking you. Has he said so? Did he roll right up to you and say, "Kate, I don't like you"? What is going on in that head of yours?'

He tightened his hold—in friendship of course.

'He frowns at me. Well, not at me when I'm looking at him, but you know how silently he gets around—someone should have found a way to make his wheels squeak by now. Anyway, sometimes I kind of sense his presence and I turn around and there he is, frowning at me.'

'You're imagining it,' Hamish said stoutly, though in his head and heart he was remembering that he spent a lot of his own time frowning at this woman when she wasn't aware of his presence. His frown was because he was pretty sure he loved her, and couldn't work out how to get past her determination to avoid love at all cost.

Could Charles also be in love with her?

Hamish could well understand if he was, and the clenching in his gut suggested he didn't like this idea one bit. Charles was far too old for her.

Not that old…

And Charles could certainly be charming…

'I'll talk to Charles,' he said firmly, and Kate laughed.

'And ask him to stop frowning at me? Oh, please!' She turned and kissed him on the cheek. 'You're a really good friend, Hamish, and I appreciate the offer, but I'll live with Charles's frowns. I only mentioned it because it happened again when we left the room after we'd been talking to him about Jack.'

She was silent for a moment, moving away a little before the settee tipped her back towards him.

'You don't suppose he thinks— He couldn't think I've got something going with Jack, could he? I mean, apart from me being far too old for Jack, he's really only interested in Megan…'

She sounded confused enough to need comfort so Hamish drew her close again, and they sat like that for a while, watching the moon come up over the horizon, spreading a silver path across the water of the cove.

'Moonlight and water—made for romance, isn't it?'

The murmured words slid seditiously into Kate's ear and her heartbeats upped their intensity, bringing heat to the innermost parts of her body.

Kissing Hamish was back!

'We can't have a romance, Hamish,' she said, betraying the words by wriggling closer to him, because being close to Hamish was extremely comforting. 'Leaving aside my hang-ups about relationships—which are huge—you're going home in a couple of weeks. It would be stupid to start something we can't finish.'

He kissed the top of her head then his lips moved down and pressed against the corner of her right eye. His tongue slid out to lick a tiny patch of skin—surely eye-skin shouldn't be erogenous.

'My leaving isn't an issue. We could finish it in Scotland. Or not finish it at all.'

Even hushed, his deep voice sent shivers down her spine. It *had* to be the accent. Daniel's voice had never made contact with her spine at all—with any of her bones, come to think of it.

'Come home with me. Be *my* family. Make a family that is ours.'

His lips had reached the corner of her mouth. He couldn't have any idea how tempting that suggestion had been—how much she longed to regain some concept of 'home' and 'family'.

Damn, she should have been concentrating on the progress of his lips, not thinking about nebulous concepts of home and family. He'd taken advantage of her distraction and was kissing her!

Perhaps she hadn't got an F for the cliff kiss…

'Are you with me on this?'

He raised his head far enough to free his lips and ask the question, but the aftershocks of the kiss were such that she couldn't answer. Bones—it was all to do with bones. His voice had affected her spine; now the kiss had made the rest of her bones turn to jelly.

Not possible.

'Apparently!' Hamish said, presumably to himself as she certainly wasn't carrying on a conversation with him. She was trying to get her bones to solidify again, and worrying about the warm feeling in the pit of her stomach that Hamish's kisses was generating.

He resumed kissing her.

She should be protesting, or at least not kissing him back, but there was something so deliciously delirious about being kissed by Hamish that shoulds and shouldn'ts didn't count.

'Oh, dear,' she managed when they drew apart to breathe some time later. 'This really shouldn't be happening, Hamish.'

'No?'

He tipped her chin up and smiled into her eyes.

'But how else can I convince you this is special? Yes, it's sudden, *and* surprising, *and* barely believable, but that doesn't mean it's not real, Kate. So I'll keep kissing you because I know words won't build the trust you need to overcome your doubts—and admit it, woman, you're kissing me right back!'

His gruff words shook her jellied bones.

'Yes, I know, and it's very nice—lovely kisses—very special, but, Hamish…'

Kate couldn't find the words she needed to tell him about the hurt inside her—about the scars so new they had no protective scabs—about the hurt against which she had so few defences.

To open herself up to pain like that again, it was unthinkable…

'No buts,' he said gently, and he kissed her again, so thoroughly she wondered if they'd leave scorch marks on the settee.

'No, I won't go to the fire on the beach with you tonight,' Kate said firmly, pushing past a lounging Hamish to get into the ED office. With Harry apparently satisfied he'd got all he could out of Jack, Kate had been shifted back to the ED for the weekend.

She'd been happy about the arrangement as there was usually less time for chat and gossip in ED—until Hamish had wandered in.

Searing embarrassment still swamped her when she remembered her behaviour on the settee the previous night. They'd eventually been startled apart by a round of applause from the kitchen, Cal announcing with unabashed delight that they'd broken the settee kissing record, set only recently by himself and Gina.

Kate had skulked off to her room, not knowing the others well enough to laugh it off, though Hamish had stayed, apparently unaffected by the fact any number of their housemates had seen them kissing.

Now here he was again, wanting her to accompany him to the fire party at the beach, making public a relationship that didn't exist.

'You'll enjoy it,' Hamish persisted.

'Yes, I will, because I'm going anyway,' Kate told him. 'With Susie. She was talking about it yesterday while she was massaging Jack's leg. And as it's in celebration of getting Megan and Jack back together, Megan's coming with us. Girls' night out.'

'Oh!' For a moment Hamish looked so downcast Kate wanted to change her mind, but when he smiled just seconds later she was glad she'd stood firm. Hamish's smiles were nearly as addictive as Hamish's kisses and neither were the kind of addiction a woman who was determined to make her own way in life could afford.

'Susie and Megan, huh? Well, that's OK.'

He wandered off, leaving Kate to get on with her work, which, today, because the ED secretary hadn't appeared, was recording patients as they came in and prioritising them to see the doctor on duty, who happened to be Charles—making it the first time Kate had worked directly with him.

She glanced cautiously around, but he was still out the back where ambulance patients were admitted or in treatment room five where a small boy who'd been vomiting all night had been shifted up ahead of a young woman with stomachache and a drunk who'd fallen out of his mate's car and taken a lot of skin off one leg.

'OK, I'll take over here while you make yourself useful out there.' Jane, a cheerful secretary who usually worked on the front desk, came bustling into the small office. 'Charles phoned to say Wendy hadn't arrived, and asked if I could come. Don't worry, I started work in this cubbyhole, so I know what to do.'

Then she nodded to the drunk who was singing a song neither Kate nor, by the looks on their faces, anyone else in the room could recognise.

'Who's your friend?'

Kate smiled.

'I'll do him first,' she said, and went out, taking the man with the gravel rash through to a treatment room. With any luck, all his leg needed was to be cleaned up and dressed, then he could go on his way.

Easier said than done. She managed to get him into the treatment room, but he'd no sooner lain down on the examination table than he gave a helpless yelp then threw up all over her.

A hastily summoned aide came in to clean up while Kate grabbed some clean scrubs and headed for the bathroom. But no matter how much water she splashed over herself, she knew she'd smell all day.

Damn the man!

Back in the treatment room, he was sitting up and at least had the decency to look embarrassed.

'Room went round and round when I lay down,' he explained, which was when she realised she'd misread his embarrassment as he began to sing again, this time about a room going round and round.

Kate shifted him so his leg was propped on an absorbent pad on the table and she could get at the bits of gravel in the wound. She flushed it first, but the grit remained embedded and she knew it was going to be a piece-by-piece job.

Using small tweezers and wearing a magnifying loupe, she painstakingly removed every grain, while her patient alternately serenaded her and asked her to marry him. She had nearly finished when Charles appeared in the doorway.

'Need me?' he said, and this time she was sure the frown accompanying the words was because of the way the two of them smelt. 'Phew! Talk about ripe!' he added, confirming her thoughts but making her smile nonetheless.

'You might like to take a look, but he's up to date with his tetanus shots, there are no deep wounds that need stitching and there's no infection, so I thought I'd swab it all over with Betadine and let him go. Leave it without a dressing to dry it out?'

'Yes,' Charles said, then he frowned again, though he should have got used to the smell by now.

He wheeled away and, because the line-up for treatment hadn't become noticeably longer, Kate finished tending her drunk then ducked over to the house to have a proper shower and change into clean clothes. She didn't want people coming into the ED and going home feeling worse than when they'd arrived.

Susie knocked on her door at eight that evening.

'You ready?' she asked, when Kate called to her to come in.

'As I'll ever be,' Kate told her. The quiet morning had turned into a hectic afternoon and she'd only come off duty fifteen minutes ago. But she'd had a quick shower and dressed in jeans and a light cotton knit sweater, thinking the breeze on the beach might be cool in spite of the fire.

'Then let's go,' Susie said, leading the way out of the house.

'Where's Megan? Weren't you going to pick her up?'

'I was, but Hamish said he had to go downtown so he said he'd get her.'

Girls' and Hamish's night out?

Had he offered deliberately? Would that explain his smile?

Kate shook her head. She was here to find her father, not to get caught up in thinking about Hamish. Not about his kisses, or his Colleague Hamish days—just to find her father.

Harry might be there tonight.

She'd ask Harry about her mother. Say she was a friend of a friend in Melbourne—from a long time ago.

'Hi you two.'

Mike and Emily greeted them, and Kate was relieved to see Emily was at last taking some time off. She worked in Theatre when Cal was operating and did shifts in other parts of the hospital, but mostly Kate had met her in the ICU where Emily had spent her free time fretting over Jack.

So her presence at the fire party was not only good for her, it meant she had at last accepted he was stable and his recovery would continue.

Susie unfolded the blanket she'd been carrying and spread it by the fire. She and Kate settled on it, though they had to move only minutes later when Megan and Hamish and Hamish's guitar arrived, all three joining Susie and Kate on the blanket that had become, in Kate's eyes, almost minuscule.

Not that Hamish was bothering her—not deliberately. Oh, no, he was being Colleague Hamish again, cheerful, chatty, making Megan laugh at silly jokes, asking her about Jackson's progress, although every member of the hospital staff personally checked Jackson's progress every day.

'He's coming home tomorrow,' Megan said happily. 'Well, home to Christina's house with me. I'm not sure how I'll manage, what with Mum over in Townsville with Dad.'

'You know we'll all do anything we can to help you with Jackson,' Susie said, putting her arm around Megan and giving her a hug. 'Anything you want, just yell, and half the staff will come running.'

Megan nodded.

'You've all been so kind—and with Jack, too, although he's still too sick for me to tell him all that happened.'

She turned to Hamish.

'Should I tell him?'

'About having Lucky at the rodeo?'

So Hamish's ability to read minds wasn't restricted to reading hers, Kate thought as Megan nodded.

But how would he reply? Kate held her breath, glad Megan hadn't asked her.

'I think you will eventually,' Hamish said. 'Not necessarily right away. But one day there'll come a time and you'll know it's the right time. Then you'll tell him and he'll understand.'

He took one of Megan's hands and held it in both of his.

'You've been very sick, too, and have been through tremendous emotional pressure, so think about yourself as well as Jack and Jackson. Do what's right for Megan sometimes, not just what's right for them—or for your parents. That's been a burden you carried on your own for far too long.'

Megan rested her head on his shoulder, and Kate heard her whispered thanks.

Kate was glad of the shadows as she blinked moisture from her eyes. Colleague Hamish was definitely something special as doctors went.

Drinks were passed around and Hamish shifted from the blanket, settling on a rock nearby and strumming lightly on his guitar. People started singing, soft ballads they'd obviously sung before, around other fires blazing on the beach. But the togetherness of it made Kate feel lost and alone again, and she remembered why she'd come on contract—and why she'd come at all.

She looked towards Hamish—strumming quietly on his rock. Could she forget her quest? Go back to Scotland with him?

Did it matter who her father was?

She no longer knew the answer to that one, and not knowing made her feel more lost than ever.

Helpless.

She waited until Susie had gone to get more wine and Megan stood up to talk to Emily and Mike, then she slipped away, heading for where the casuarina trees threw shadows across the top of the beach—shadows deep enough to hide her departure.

'Leaving so early? I'll walk you home.'

Brian's voice came from the very deepest of the shadows and, certain she hadn't seen him approaching as she'd walked up the beach, she wondered if he'd been standing there.

Watching…

A shiver she didn't understand feathered down her spine, and when Hamish spoke from close behind her, she was so relieved she nearly flew into his arms.

'Sorry, had to say goodbye to Mike,' he said, catching up with her and slipping his arm around her waist. 'Oh, hi, Brian! You going down to join the party?'

'Well, I was but then I saw Kate leaving and thought I'd walk her home.'

'Kind of you, but I'd already offered. You go and join the fun.' Hamish's arm tightened, drawing Kate closer to his body.

'Oh, well, I guess I might as well,' Brian said, and he walked slowly out of the shadows towards the beach.

Reluctantly, because standing hip to hip with Hamish was very comforting, Kate drew away from her rescuer.

'I might have wanted to walk home with Brian,' she told him, angry because she couldn't handle the way Hamish changed from colleague to, well, some kind of lover with such consummate ease.

'You could have said so,' Hamish pointed out. 'You could have said, "Thanks but, no, thanks, Hamish, I'm going home with Brian."'

'I wouldn't have gone *home* with Brian,' Kate retorted. 'Not the way you make it sound.'

'Even to avoid me? Because that's what you're doing, isn't it, Kate?'

She heard his pain but had to argue.

'It's best that way.'

Hamish put his arm around her and drew her close again.

'Is it? I don't think so. And is it just me you're avoiding or are you afraid to let anyone, even colleagues, get close to you in case you're hurt again? Is that why you walked away from the fire? Is that why you've suddenly got doubts about finding your father?'

'That's ridiculous! You don't know that!' Kate snapped, irritated beyond reason by too many sensations ricocheting through her body.

And by the fact he always seemed to get things right!

He was holding her just lightly enough that she knew she could break away.

If she wanted to...

'Don't I?' He drew her just slightly closer. 'Oh, Kate!' he sighed. 'You've every right to feel vulnerable, but is hiding away from emotion the answer? You're braver than that, Kate. You're a fighter. I saw you in action with Jack.'

She didn't feel like a fighter. She felt like a wimp—weak and feeble, and nervy from the touch of this man's hands. All she wanted was to lean against him and feel his lips on hers, and let the sensations of a kiss drive all the demons from her mind.

She was obviously quite, quite mad!

She moved away from him, remembering avoidance, but he tugged her closer, then somehow they were in the darkest shadows, and he was kissing her again, kissing her with such ferocious intensity she couldn't breathe, let alone think.

'I know you've got a good heart that reaches out to touch all those around you,' he said, what seemed like hours but was probably only minutes later. 'And I know you've been immeasurably hurt by people you loved and by circumstances beyond your control. I understand your fear, my Kateling, but your kisses tell me something else. So if you want me to stop kissing you, then...'

Kate heard his words coming to her through a fog of well-being, and she leaned against the man who still held her in his arms.

'You'll have to tell me!' he said crossly, tucking her closer and pressing his lips against her hair. 'You'll have to stop kissing me back.'

'Not tonight,' she whispered. 'Let's, just for tonight, forget about everything else and kiss again. Maybe we'll get sick of it—like chocolate if you have too much.'

She felt his chest move as he chuckled, then his hands clasped her head, tilting it up again so his lips could claim hers.

Stupid in the heart, she told herself when, drunk with kisses, they turned and, arm in arm, walked back towards the house.

'I'll leave you at your door,' Hamish announced, as they climbed the front steps. 'I don't know about you, but the chocolate analogy didn't work for me. However, I've always had one guiding principle that fits most situations, and that's never to make a decision at night. An idea that after a few pints is absolutely foolproof and bound to bring in millions is often revealed as flawed in the sober light of day and, though I don't want to equate women with bright ideas, the same rule works with relationships.'

'Or non-relationships, as the case may be,' Kate whispered, thankful she didn't have to make a decision because the desire humming through her body made thinking nigh impossible.

But, true to his word, he left her at her door, Colleague Hamish back again, placing a chaste kiss on her forehead before opening her door for her and wishing her goodnight, his deep voice with the soft Scots burr making magic of the simple words.

Kate shut her door and leaned against it. She heard his footsteps going along the passageway, bypassing his door, growing fainter as he walked through the kitchen. Was she imagining she could hear the springs on the old settee squeaking?

Was he sitting out there now?

Regretting his gallantry at leaving her at her door?

Half expecting her to join him?

Her body remembered the electric charge their kisses had

generated, and yearned for the release and forgetfulness that spending a night with Hamish would surely bring.

But it would only be for a night and after that—awkwardness, embarrassment, regret. All of those and more—the big one—guilt, because casual sex wasn't her way.

Worse, guilt because he was far too nice a man to use that way.

Kate shook her head, changed into pyjamas and climbed into her lonely bed.

Hamish slumped down onto the settee—again.

He was obviously mad!

Leaving Kate at the door like that—going all gentlemanly when what he should have done was ease the two of them through that bedroom door and let nature resolve the fragile barriers Kate kept erecting between them.

He held his head in his hands and applied pressure to his skull with his fingers, though it wasn't his brain that was hurting.

It was all the rest of him, hurting in a way he'd never felt before—like an all-over cramp, which proved all the rot you read about love being joyous and uplifting was totally wrong. Love hurt like hell, that was what love did.

If it *was* love, not some as yet unidentified tropical disease.

Don't joke about it, this is serious, he told the flippant self that had, up till then, ruled the emotional part of his life.

But if he couldn't joke, how else to handle it?

Grown men didn't cry.

Though he didn't feel like crying. He felt like hitting something, like raging and ranting and yelling at whatever callous Fate had decreed he fall in love right here and right now.

Not only fall in love, but fall in love with probably the only woman on the entire planet who had excellent, viable, irrefutable reasons for not loving him back!

Well, there were probably quite a few women who wouldn't want him. But only one he wanted…

* * *

Sunday in the ED was far quieter than Kate had expected it to be. Hamish, who was on duty elsewhere in the hospital, drifted in, in search of Mrs Grubb's chocolate-chip cookies, which he swore he could smell somewhere on the premises. He explained that people in country towns really didn't like bothering doctors on a Sunday.

'Or perhaps they don't like giving up their Sundays for minor medical problems when they can just as easily take Monday off work and bother doctors then,' Kate suggested, and Hamish tutted.

'So young to be so cynical! It seems you've got out of the city just in time. But you're right in one thing—Monday is always frantically busy.'

'My day off,' Kate said smugly, pleased to be handling what could have been an awkward post-kissing conversation with Hamish so well. Or maybe it was Hamish who was directing it so well…

But she kept up her end. 'Monday and Tuesday this week, then back in ED again from Wednesday through to Saturday,' she explained with a lot of false cheer.

'But you'll miss the rodeo,' Hamish protested. 'You're working this weekend—shouldn't you be off next weekend?'

Kate shrugged off his concern.

'I'm a contract worker, and I said when I was employed I'd be happy to work weekend shifts,' she explained, not adding that she'd thought having weekdays off would be more advantageous in her search.

What search?

Hamish leaned against a convenient wall and studied her.

'My decision in the sober light of day was that I was wrong in my decision last night,' he said quietly, and Kate had to smile.

'So the chocolate-chip cookie search was a scam.'

'Not entirely. They're here somewhere—but I did want to see you.'

'And having seen me?'

'I thought I'd put a proposition to you. Let's talk to Charles—no one else—about your family.'

'But Charles grew up at Wetherby Downs—that's hundreds of miles away from here.'

'OK, scrap Charles—talk to Harry. He'll be discreet. He can find out what you need to know then you can decide whether or not you still want to make contact with your father.'

Kate stared at him.

'What are you talking about? Why wouldn't I want to make contact with my father?'

He smiled—the gentle smile that curled around his lips and lurked so sympathetically in his eyes. Yet he couldn't *know* that the rash, grief-laden impetus that had propelled her thousands of miles north had turned to doubt and dread.

'I imagine because it finally entered your admittedly beautiful head that maybe a middle-aged man might not want an unknown daughter turning up on his doorstep.'

He came closer and took her hand.

'I know you care about people, Kate. Care deeply for those you love. That's been obvious since I first met you. So it's not so hard to take the next step and imagine how disturbed you must be feeling about disrupting the life of a man you don't know but might want to care about. Of course you're wondering and worrying about the damage your appearance in his life might do, not only to him but to his entire family. And, being Kate, you're prepared to sacrifice your own happiness in order to not disturb his—whoever he might be.'

Kate stared at Hamish, unable to believe this man could so easily read the thoughts that had been festering in her head all week. To the extent that when she'd gone to the library one morning and found old electoral rolls, she hadn't been unduly disappointed when she hadn't found her mother's name—or any voters with the same surname.

'Go find the cookies!' she snapped at him, snatching her hands from his grasp and moving crossly away. 'I hope they make you fat!'

He was right, of course, which was what had made her angry—him being right plus the fact that her mind was now so muddled she was barely aware which way was up.

And most of the muddle was Hamish-oriented.

The more doubts she had about finding her father, the more appealing the idea of a trip to Scotland sounded.

She could always come back. What was one more broken heart?

Are you mad? Of course you don't want to take that risk!

A loud, demanding car horn cut through her helplessly circling thoughts and she went through to the ambulance bay to meet it, arriving in time to see Georgie Turner pull up on her motorbike behind the car.

'Bed, Kate. One of my patients about to pop.'

An orderly had already wheeled a bed out to the car, and Grace, who'd been dozing in a treatment room, also appeared.

'This patient's mine,' she said to Kate, helping Georgie settle the woman on the bed. 'Love deliveries, love babies, and, besides, I'm on duty in the nursery this week so I deserve to be the first to meet this little person.'

'You're so clucky it's a wonder you don't lay eggs,' Georgie said to Grace, and, with the help of the husband, the two of them took their patient through to the birthing suites.

'I'll shift your car and bring you the keys,' Kate told the husband, who looked too stunned to really take in what she'd said, but as the keys were dangling from the ignition, it didn't matter.

Kate parked the car safely in the car park and took the keys in, arriving in time to see the new life emerge into the world. A little girl to take Jackson's place in the nursery. She looked at the love and wonder on the faces of all those present—even that of Georgie, who must deliver a dozen babies a month.

Everyone loved a newborn—but a new daughter who was twenty-seven?

She made her way back to the ED. So far, coming to Crocodile Creek had thrown up more questions than it had answers.

CHAPTER EIGHT

'BATMAN AND ROBIN ride again.'

Hamish's voice startled Kate out of a reverie about the man who had spoken—a man she'd been avoiding, and about whom she definitely should not be thinking!

But though he'd made the joking comment, the coolness in his voice told her he was well aware of her avoidance tactics. And perhaps that he'd been hurt by them.

She glanced at him, but his face gave nothing away. Still, somehow, deep inside she hoped she hadn't hurt him.

Hamish didn't deserve that.

'Why are you doing this flight?' she asked, her work self ignoring all the palaver going on in her head. 'Mike's flying and you're not on call.'

'Mike's got that twenty-four-hour bug that's been going around. Rex is flying, and the patient's a child, so why not me?'

Hamish spoke with such exaggerated patience that Kate wanted to grind her teeth.

Batman probably wasn't a tooth grinder, but Batman probably didn't get collywobbles in his stomach when he got into the Batmobile with Robin.

With a decidedly unfriendly, though meticulously polite, Robin!

'The patient's a child?'

'Out on Wallaby Island.' Hamish nodded his confirmation. 'Apparently the silly kid disobeyed his parents and went wandering out on the reef without protection on his feet.'

'And?' Kate prompted, hoping to get more of the story before they took off.

'Walked on a stonefish.'

'A stonefish? What on earth's a stonefish? A fish that eats stones?'

Hamish turned and his cold demeanour cracked to the extent she was sure a small smile slipped out, then quickly disappeared.

Kate felt the chain reaction of quivery delight along the nerves throughout her body, even though what she thought had been a smile might just have been a grimace.

But the quivery delight reminded her why she'd been avoiding him.

'You're the Aussie and you don't know what a stonefish is?'

His question jerked her back to business, and she was about to remind him she was a city person when Rex handed them headsets then began take-off procedures. It was easier to wait until they were in the air to pursue the conversation.

'A stonefish?' she prompted Hamish.

Bad move as he smiled at her again, a real smile this time, but quivery delight was soon replaced by concern as he explained.

'It's a nasty beastie that looks very like a largish rock. It hides among other largish rocks, so unsuspecting prey rests on it then gets poisoned by venom from one of the glands along the dorsal fin spines.'

'That's unbelievable!' Kate muttered. 'I mean, I know we have a good range of poisonous snakes and spiders, but I thought, apart from sharks and stinging jellyfish, the seas were fairly safe. Is it bad venom? Do people die?'

'Never in Australia, although there are recorded cases of deaths overseas.'

It was Rex who provided this answer, then Hamish took up the explanations.

'The venom can have nerve, muscle, vascular and myocardial effects. We have antivenin, and normally there's some in the medical kit out at the island, but apparently when they looked at it, it was out of date.'

'Oh, for heaven's sake, doesn't anyone check these things?' Kate muttered. 'Cal insisted we check the medical kits in isolated places when I did a clinic flight with him. Isn't there a rule that the person with the key to the kit has to check it?'

Hamish nodded.

'Unfortunately, they've had so much trouble with the kit at Wallaby Island, Charles has been thinking of removing it. The island is only a twenty-minute flight away— Look, you can see it now.'

Kate peered out the window at the rounded shape of the island, jutting out of the azure sea, the waters around it paler shades of translucent green.

'That's the reef,' Hamish explained. 'One of the reasons Wallaby is so popular as a tourist destination is the magnificent fringing reef.'

But although she was stunned by the beauty of the place they were approaching, she was more worried about the child who'd been stung by the stonefish.

Hamish must have been just as worried. The moment they touched down, he was out of his seat, unstrapping a small backpack, another backpack that contained resuscitation gear and the lightweight stretcher.

'I'll yell if we need the stretcher,' he said to Rex, who had come through to open the door. 'Come on,' he added to Kate, dropping out of the chopper then racing, doubled over, to where a small group of people was clustered beside the helipad.

The child, eight or nine, Kate judged, was sitting, white-faced, on his mother's knee, an oxygen mask on his face and one foot in a bucket of water.

Beside the pair, a young man wearing a bright Hawaiian-print shirt stood uncertainly. A second man detached himself from the group and headed towards the helicopter.

Hamish nodded at the young man, acknowledging his presence but at the same time conveying the utmost disapproval.

'That's Kurt,' he muttered to Kate. 'Wallaby Island's current keeper of the medical kit. At least he's done something right, with the hot water.'

'Hot water?' Kate echoed.

'The pressure immobilisation we use for most venoms is useless with stonefish. In fact, it can worsen the pain,' Hamish explained as he knelt beside the child. 'Immersing the injured part in hot water—forty to forty-five degrees—is the best thing to do until we can get some antivenin and regional anaesthetic into the patient.'

He'd let his pack slide to the ground and Kate put hers down beside it, grateful resus equipment wasn't needed. She opened the one Hamish had carried, while Hamish introduced himself to the boy—Jason—and his mother, Julie.

'It hurts so much,' the boy whimpered.

Kate found the ampoules of stonefish antivenin easily enough. She broke one open and filled a syringe, while Hamish checked the child, asking questions about allergies and examining the wound.

'We'll need another ampoule of the antivenin, Kate,' he said quietly. 'We use one for every two puncture wounds and young Jason here has managed to tread on four of the beastie's thirteen spikes.'

'This is going to hurt when I prick you, Jason, but it won't be nearly as bad as the pain from that rotten stonefish, so just hang onto Mum for me while I get it in.'

He injected the antivenin into the muscle on Jason's thigh,

and though the boy did no more than wince at the injection, his mother's face lost colour and Kate put out a hand to hold her steady.

'Not much good around needles,' Julie said weakly, smiling her thanks at Kate.

'I don't know anyone who is,' Kate told her.

'OK, now we'll see what we can do to stop some of that pain, young Jason,' Hamish said. 'Kate, you'll see a pack with a sterile syringe of bupivacaine in there somewhere,' he said. 'Twenty mils at 25 per cent. That'll provide a regional block, which works better in these cases than narcotic analgesics.'

Kate found the pack he needed and handed it to him. She watched the child, and Hamish handling him—so gently competent Kate could see why paediatrics should be his specialty.

'I'll get this into him and we'll check him out while it's working. A couple of minutes at this stage won't make a difference.'

Check out the mother, too, Kate thought, noticing for the first time that Julie was pregnant.

Hamish was asking her if Jason was on any medication, and Julie was answering calmly enough, but a flutter of fear trembled beneath the words and revealed itself in the tremor of the hands that rested lightly on her son's shoulders.

'We'll take you both back to the mainland,' Hamish said, when Kate had finished jotting down Jason's details on the initial assessment form. 'Stonefish toxin can affect many parts of the body, so we need to keep an eye on Jason, at least overnight. We also need to treat the wounds themselves. I want an X-ray to make sure no fragments of the spines broke off in his foot, and it's possible he'll need antibiotics if the wounds become infected.'

'What about my husband?' Julie asked. 'He went off on a fishing trip early this morning—he doesn't know about this. What will he do?'

'Do you want us to let him know? We can radio the fishing boat,' Kurt offered.

Julie thought about it for a moment, then turned to Hamish. 'Should I let him know?'

Kate knew the question behind the question was, *Is my son's life in danger?* And she silently applauded Julie's courage in asking it.

'We'll watch Jason carefully for any signs the venom is affecting him. The resort has a small helicopter and I'm sure if you needed your husband urgently, they would fly him over, but the decision about whether you tell him now or later is up to you.'

Kurt nodded his agreement, adding they could always airlift him off the fishing boat.

'Then let him enjoy his day out,' Julie said. 'He'll be angry I didn't contact him but he's been working far too hard and been under a lot of stress. He needs whatever relaxation he can get.'

'The fishing trip gets back in time for him to take this afternoon's flight back to the mainland,' Kurt offered. 'I'll get the housemaid to pack up your things, then I'll meet the fishing boat and tell Mr Anstead what's happened. Our agent in Crocodile Creek can meet the chopper and take him to the hospital.'

Hamish nodded his approval of this arrangement, though he was still furious with Kurt for neglecting to keep the contents of the medical kit up to date.

'OK, let's get you into the helicopter, young Jason,' he said, reaching down, removing the oxygen mask and lifting the child into his arms. Kate had already slung one backpack across her shoulders and she carried the second as she herded an anxious Julie across the helipad.

And though 98 per cent of Hamish's concentration was on his patient—feeling the steady rise and fall of the child's chest against his, watching the throb of a pulse beneath Jason's chin—

the other two per cent had been enticed into consideration of Kate—and the way she'd been avoiding him for the last few days.

Perhaps it was for the best. He could understand her reluctance to get involved again, yet he couldn't clear his head of the daft idea that she was the only woman in the world for him.

He, who had never believed in such nonsense! As if there would only be one perfect match for every person in the world!

But the deep ache inside him gave lie to his argument. It told him there was only one person in the world for him.

Kate…

'Want to sit up front?' he asked Jason, knowing young children who didn't need mechanical support or monitoring were usually happier if they could ride up front.

'Yes please.'

Jason's response was so wholehearted Hamish was reassured that his initial assessment of the child—that he hadn't taken in a huge dose of venom—had been correct. Whether the stonefish was immature or Jason's bodyweight was so light the spines didn't penetrate deeply, Hamish didn't know, but apart from the excruciating pain Jason hadn't shown any of the toxic effects of stonefish venom.

So far!

Rex helped him settle the boy into the copilot's seat, and pointed out what all the controls did.

'You can help me fly it if you like,' Rex offered. 'Just hold on here and do what I do.'

He fitted a pair of headphones to the small head.

Kate, who was helping Julie fasten her seat belt, looked towards the cockpit with alarm, and Hamish smiled. As far as he knew, she hadn't ridden up front on a flight yet, so wouldn't realise the second set of controls wasn't effective unless a special switch was thrown.

Hamish handed Julie a second pair of earphones.

'Here. You can talk to Jason through the mouthpiece.' He

pointed to the small attachment, then passed Kate one of the white helmets she'd worn on her first flight—helmets that held both earphones and a microphone.

A microphone so those in the helicopter could converse without shouting, yet it couldn't help him talk to Kate—even if they'd been alone. You couldn't talk to someone who didn't want to hear.

Charles met them at the helipad.

'The boy all right?' he asked Hamish, as Kate helped Julie out of the chopper and Rex lifted Jason out, settling him on the stretcher two orderlies had waiting nearby.

'You get a ride to the hospital, kid!' Rex said, and Hamish saw the look of hero-worship in Jason's eyes.

'I liked the helicopter best,' he assured Rex, and Hamish nodded to Charles.

'Yes, I think the boy's all right,' he said, 'but we're going to have to do something about the medical kit at Wallaby. They don't deserve to have it there if the person in charge can't be bothered to check it regularly.'

'I'll go over myself later this week and sort it out,' Charles promised, then he frowned, not at Hamish's concern but at Kate, who was walking beside Jason on his wheeled stretcher.

It was the first time Hamish had ever noticed this reaction— the frown Kate had mentioned to him before she'd started avoiding him.

'She's a good nurse—very empathetic,' he told Charles, although he knew Kate wouldn't thank him for sticking up for her.

Charles turned his frown on Hamish.

'Do you think I don't know that?' he demanded.

Frowns all round! Hamish was sure one was gathering on his forehead.

'You were frowning at her,' he pointed out, then saw a look of sadness cross Charles's face.

'Frowning at my own bitter thoughts, Hamish, not at your Kate.'

'She's not *my* Kate!' Hamish snapped, and he walked away, moving swiftly to catch up with the cavalcade of stretcher, patient, mother and nurse, which was now inside the hospital grounds.

He tagged along as they entered the ED, in time to ask the orderlies to take Jason straight to a treatment room. He could use a portable X-ray machine to check for spines in his foot, then debride the wounds and dress them. If he had to operate to remove pieces of spine, it was a minor procedure and could be done in the treatment room.

She'd never be his Kate, unless he could come up with a miracle.

Grace met them as they came in, introducing herself to Jason and explaining she'd be helping Dr Hamish look after him.

Hamish caught the look that passed between Kate and Grace. Was Kate really so worried about propinquity between them that she'd enlisted Grace's help in avoiding him?

The thought saddened the two per cent of his brain he was allowing to linger with Kate, but as he followed Grace into the small treatment room he pushed even that small portion aside. Jason deserved one hundred per cent.

'We'll be banished from the room while they take the X-ray,' Kate said to Julie. 'Would you like a cup of tea or coffee?'

'Please!' Julie said. 'Weak tea with plenty of milk. I'm trying to totally avoid caffeine but I think I deserve a cuppa today.'

Kate sent an aide to get tea and biscuits, then settled Julie on a chair outside the treatment room.

'When's the baby due?'

Julie turned to her with a puzzled expression, then pressed a hand to her stomach.

'Do you know, I'd almost forgotten about the baby!' She patted her bulge as if apologising to it. 'I'm thirty-two weeks. My husband had a week off and we took the opportunity to take a holiday before the baby arrived. Heaven knows when we'll get away again once we're a family of four.'

Kate waited with Julie until Hamish was satisfied he'd cleaned out Jason's wounds and the boy could be transferred to the children's room, so called because it looked more like a magical playroom than a hospital ward.

'I want to watch him overnight,' Hamish explained to Julie, 'and start him on a course of oral steroids. The antivenin is made from horse serum and in some cases can cause serum sickness. The steroids guard against that happening.'

'Aren't steroids bad for kids?' Julie asked.

'Only if they're taking them to improve their sports performance,' Hamish teased. 'We're not talking massive doses—fifty milligrams of prednisolone daily for five days. It's a drug used often for children—particularly those with chronic asthma. We'll divide the dose into three so he takes three tablets a day.'

Julie accompanied Jason and Hamish to the children's room, but Kate caught up with her later that day when she finished work and went to see how her small patient was faring.

Bad move as Hamish was there, but Kate was happy to see Jason's father had arrived and was to spend the night with his son, while Julie went to the hotel to rest.

'I think we connect more to patients we bring in on emergency flights,' Hamish said, walking with her out of the hospital.

Kate nodded, but didn't answer. It didn't seem to matter how much she avoided Hamish, because the instant he was back in her presence again all the attraction came roaring back to life, made stronger rather than diminished by her stringent avoidance tactics.

Did he know she always walked back through the garden that he guided her that way?

It was early evening, the moon not yet risen, and though bright stars threw mellow light the path was darkly shadowed.

'I'm sorry I left you at your door on Saturday night,' he said.

It was the last thing Kate had expected to hear, although he had said something similar before. She stopped—quite close to the ginger plant, for she could smell the flowers—and looked at her companion.

'Why?'

Hamish drew a deep breath. If he told her he loved her, would it destroy the very fragile thread that linked them?

Or was he imagining even that?

But for days he'd gone along with her avoidance tactics, thinking space might clear his brain, but all it had done had been to confuse him even further.

And if she'd asked Grace to help her avoid him? Well, that hurt!

He took another breath.

'Because if I hadn't we'd have made love, and maybe, during love-making, if I'd told you I loved you, it might have meant more than baldly coming out with it in a garden with no moonlight and that damned ginger plant overwhelming me with its perfume.'

'It is rather strong,' Kate remarked, and Hamish wondered if she'd even heard his declaration.

He was no good at this. He was good at detached. Very good at flippant. Heartfelt declarations of love were too new. Even thinking about them, practising what he had to say, had made him feel raw and exposed.

Now he'd messed things up with the ginger plant.

Had he actually said the love bit? Had he told her?

If he had, she showed no inclination to reply, merely walking a little further along the path.

He followed, feeling like Rudolph when he'd had a scolding.

'Well?' he demanded. Rudolph would have barked.

Much better at flippant!

But the cramp was back, and his knees were shaking, and he knew flippant wasn't any use to him at all.

He steadied himself, took hold of her elbows and looked down into her shadowed eyes.

'I love you, Kate,' he repeated, just in case he hadn't said it earlier.

Or she hadn't heard it.

'I know, Hamish,' she whispered. 'But I don't know how to answer you. I'm just so confused.'

It wasn't much but Hamish felt considerably heartened.

'Let's go to dinner at the Athina and talk about it. Talk it through. There has to be an answer to this somewhere. Besides, you haven't been there—it's the most ro—' he caught himself just in time '—beautiful place. Mike's parents own and run it.'

He took her hands, lifted them to his lips and kissed her knuckles one by one. Would physical contact strengthen his invitation? He took more heart from the fact she didn't draw away, but even in the shadows he saw her shake her head.

Anger came so swiftly he had no time to stem it!

'You didn't say no to a trip to the pub with Harry last night.'

The accusation hung in the air between them, then Kate said softly, 'There's no danger in a drink with Harry at the pub. And we were celebrating the fact that Jack's off the hook. Todd and Digger have been arrested, and because Jack's agreed to testify against them and Digger's story backs up Jack's, it means he's free and clear. It was a celebration.'

'Dinner with me could be a celebration!' he snapped, angry beyond reason, although her explanation had made sense.

'We've nothing to celebrate,' she reminded him.

'Because you won't give in.' He was speaking far too loudly, but the hot rush of emotion welling inside him refused to be capped. 'You must feel something for me, or you wouldn't be avoiding me. You'd be treating me the way you treat Cal, or Mike, or—dare I say it?—bloody Harry! But you're not. You've even got Grace helping you—'

'Grace? Helping me what?'

'Helping you avoid me.'

He knew as he said the words they were wrong. Kate was such a private person there was no way she would have talked about her feelings to Grace, or anyone else.

He wanted to unsay it, but it was too late.

The thread—real or imaginary—had surely broken.

Or had it?

Kate had taken back her hands but she hadn't moved away.

He tamped down the still smouldering anger and took her in his arms, holding her close, reminding himself that this emotional vulnerability was probably far harder for her than it was for him.

Although he couldn't imagine it!

He took a steadying breath and tried another tack.

'Did you ask Harry about your mother?'

The movement of her head against his chest told him she hadn't.

'For some reason?'

A nod this time.

'Still having second thoughts, Kate?'

She edged away and looked up at him, a pathetic attempt at a smile trembling on her lips.

'And third and fourth and fifth thoughts, Hamish,' she said quietly. 'Does it matter? Do I really care? I don't know any more.'

She kissed him gently on the lips then drew away again.

'I was running on emotion as I headed north. The idea of finding my father helped me set aside things I couldn't cope with—grief and loss and anger. And I believed having something to do—a quest—would give me time to arm myself in some way—build defences to protect myself against hurt like that again.'

Another kiss brushed against his lips.

'Then I met you, before the defences were in place—and that's terrifying, Hamish.'

He held her closer, wrapping her tightly in his arms, desperate to protect her from the hurt she feared, his own hurt and anger forgotten in the rush of love engulfing him.

She nestled against him.

'I know I've hurt you these last few days, avoiding you the way I have, but it was only to avoid a greater hurt later on.'

Hamish kissed the top of her head.

'To borrow your own word—piffle!' he said, sounding more like a frog than a prince as emotion choked the words on their way out. 'Greater happiness, that's all there'll be later on. We'll work it out.'

'Will we?' she asked, moving away. 'I don't think so.'

'Well I do!' he said, releasing the reins on both anger and flippancy.

There were times when only they would do.

'But I'd like you to know this is not exactly a walk in the park for me,' he grumbled. 'How do you think I'm feeling— thirty years of age and finding myself in the clutches of the phenomenon I've scoffed at all my adult life? Romantic love, I've pontificated—usually after several single malts—is an illusion, perpetuated through the ages by merchants with a winning way with words. Think back to the seers and witches who sold love potions—it's always been a commercial con.'

He paused, looking down into her face and brushing her hair back from her forehead.

Could she feel the change in him? Guess how just looking at her made him feel?

How to explain?

'And until one afternoon a couple of weeks ago, I believed this foolishness,' he said quietly. 'Until one afternoon, when a sunbeam shone on a brown curl and turned it gold…'

He knew he sounded strained, and though he'd tried to make light of his emotions, Kate must have heard his pain. She reached up and kissed him on the lips, her kiss denying all the things she'd said. Passion, deep and hot and hard, stirred his blood until he could feel it thrumming through his veins.

CHAPTER NINE

'I CAN'T BELIEVE you did all that organising for the rodeo then opted to work the day it was on,' Kate said, looking at the man who'd come lounging into the Emergency Department in search of distraction.

Hamish shrugged broad shoulders in a gesture so familiar she couldn't believe she wouldn't be seeing it for ever.

'The others will all have an ongoing relationship with Wygera and the people out there. I leave next week and probably won't ever see them again.'

He sounded regretful, but it wasn't regret that tightened Kate's stomach when he talked about leaving. It was like the shoulder shrug. The familiarity. And a lot of things she didn't want to think about.

Except that she did.

Most of the time...

So, she could go to Scotland with him. The offer was there...

But it would take a leap faith and she didn't have much faith these days.

Except when she was kissing him...

Or he was kissing her...

'Besides,' he continued, for once not attuned to her thoughts, 'you weren't going to be there and if you ask me which I'd prefer—a rodeo without Kate or a hospital with her—then there's no choice.'

Uh-oh, maybe he was attuned to her thoughts...

He spread his arms wide and smiled at her.

'Stop it!' she snapped, glad the place was as quiet as a tomb so no one heard her. The entire population of Crocodile Creek must be out at the rodeo.

'Stop what?'

Dark blue eyes projected injured innocence, making Kate madder than ever.

'Stop smiling at me. And talking like that. You know I don't want a relationship.'

His smile became gentler.

'Don't you, Kate?' he said, then he put his hands on her shoulders and drew her closer.

'Don't you?' he repeated as his lips closed on hers.

'Don't you?' he breathed, a long time later, when they drew apart to catch their breath.

'Don't do this, Hamish,' she murmured brokenly, shaking her head to emphasise her words. 'I really, really, really don't want this.'

'Only because you've been hurt—because everything you knew and believed in turned out to be a lie. But this isn't a lie, Kate. Deep down in your heart you must know it's more than a passing fancy—more than physical attraction or lust or whatever other excuse you make to yourself to fend me off.'

She looked at him and shook her head, but before she could reply Mike burst through the door.

'You two on call for the Rescue Service?'

Kate nodded.

'Do you need us both?' Hamish asked.

'I think so. Multi-vehicle traffic accident up on the pass. The ambulance is on the way. It was at the rodeo and left from there. The rodeo's over and the hospital staff who were out there are all on their way back here, so this place won't be short-staffed for long.'

'I'll just let someone know we're going,' Kate told him. 'It's been so slow today I've been restocking the dressing cupboard and sent the others off for a second afternoon tea. Mrs Grubb's been baking chocolate-chip cookies, so they didn't need to be persuaded.'

Kate whisked away, and Hamish watched her go.

'Not winning her over?' Mike said, and Hamish turned back to his friend.

'*What* did you say?'

Mike laughed.

'Come on, mate. You must know the whole hospital is talking about you and Kate. The staff have been laying bets on how long you'd take to—well, to get her into bed.'

'They'd better not have been!' Hamish growled. 'How dare they talk about her that way?'

Mike touched his arm.

'Relax,' he said. 'You know how it happens. It doesn't belittle you or Kate. If anything, it shows the affection in which people hold you. And sometimes it also shows how stupid we are when it comes to love. Apparently Walter Grubb was running a book down at the Black Cockatoo on when Emily and I would get together—and that was years before we finally did.'

Mike's lack of concern over the groundsman's behaviour cooled Hamish's anger—slightly. Walter Grubb had better not be running a book on him at the local pub.

Though maybe he should take whatever odds Walter was offering on him losing her.

Because, in spite of the passion of Kate's kisses, and the heat that roared between them, he *was* losing her. Or maybe not winning her was a better way to put it, as she'd never really been his to begin with.

He followed Mike out to the chopper, wondering what she'd been about to say when Mike had walked in—knowing in his heart it had been another rejection.

So why didn't he give up?

He couldn't, that was why. Somewhere deep inside him was a certainty that Kate was his future, and all the avoidance, and denial, and, yes, joking in the world couldn't kill that notion.

He glared at the woman in question as she arrived at the helipad. She took her overalls from Mike, chatting away as if she hadn't a care in the world.

Which she had—lots of cares—so it just proved how much better she was at hiding her emotions than he was!

Growling quietly to himself because, distracted, he'd stepped into the wrong leg of his overalls, he turned his mind from Kate to what lay ahead.

'Where's the accident?' he asked Mike. 'Right at the top of the pass, or further down?'

'Further down. There's a lay-by about a kilometre from the top where I can land. Apparently a fully loaded cattle road train lost its brakes coming down, and as it crossed the road to go up the safety ramp it struck a vehicle coming from the other direction.'

'A fully loaded cattle train? You're talking three trailers? A hundred head of cattle, many dead or injured, the others loose on the highway? Anything could happen.'

'And probably will,' Mike said.

The flight was short, but as they came into land in the fading daylight they could see the chaos beneath them. Dead and dying cattle lay across the road, policemen with rifles shooting those beyond saving.

'Pity we're not vets,' Kate muttered, wincing as Mike opened the door and another shot rang out.

'We'll have enough injured people to worry about,' Hamish said, but Kate, seeing the mangled cabins of two semi-trailers, was doubtful. The fire brigade's crash unit was already on the scene and men with giant tin snips were cutting at the tangled metal.

'Have you got anyone out?' Hamish asked, as Harry joined them by the side of the road.

'Not yet,' Harry said, his voice not hopeful. 'The smaller semi is the Alcotts'—the people who supplied the rodeo bulls. They had four bulls at the rodeo so presumably there are four in the trailer. We haven't looked at them yet—too busy trying to clear the cattle from the other wreck off the road.'

He shook his head then left, answering a call from one of his men.

'Let's see what we can in the cabins,' Mike suggested, and the three of them headed for the centre of the action, Kate and Hamish carrying bags, while Mike had the lightweight stretcher.

The prime mover of the cattle train had ridden right over the smaller vehicle so it was hard to see where one ended and the other began.

'One more cut and you'll be able to get at the bloke up the top,' one of the fire crew told them, and they stood back to let the experts work. 'Once he's out, we can cut through to the other vehicle, though it doesn't look too good for anyone in it.'

The cattle train driver was barely conscious but responded both to Hamish's voice and to sensory stimulation. Aware they had to get him out before attempts could be made to rescue anyone else, Hamish worked swiftly, starting oxygen, protecting the man's neck with a cervical collar, sliding a short spine board behind him and securing it so they could lift him out in a sitting position without moving his spine more than necessary.

Within minutes they had him on the ground, well away from the firemen who were continuing their efforts to untangle the two vehicles with the jaws of life and a small crane attached to their unit.

Hamish worked with his usual thoroughness and Kate

thought what a loss he'd be to emergency services when he began his paediatric specialty.

In Scotland...

'Breathing OK, carotid pulse strong, BP 149 over 80, high but not disastrous, no sign of tension pneumothorax or flail chest, minor contusions without too much blood loss, no facial injuries indicative of hitting the windscreen, no obvious damage to his skull—but he'll need scans—damage to left patella, broken right tib and fib.' Hamish was listing the injuries while Kate did the documentation and Mike started an IV infusion. 'That's all I can see, and he's stable enough to move. Let's get him to the chopper. Mike can take him back to town while we wait to see if they get someone out of the other vehicle. The ambulance should be here soon. We'll ride back in that.'

Kate looked over at the flattened cabin and wondered if it could be possible for someone to have survived. She carried the bag of fluid while the men carried the stretcher back to the helicopter, then waited while Mike and Hamish secured their patient inside.

'Get Harry to radio if you need me back here,' Mike said, then he shut the door and Hamish steered Kate away before the rotors started moving. A tow truck had arrived, its winch lifting dead cattle off the road, but back at the scene of the accident a very much alive animal bellowed for release from the trailer that held the rodeo bulls.

'We've checked,' Harry said. 'Although the Alcotts had four bulls at the rodeo, the only passenger in the trailer is this huge fellow—I think he's the one they call Oscar. He's stamping and pawing and bellowing like crazy, but I daren't let him out without someone here who knows how to handle him.' He frowned in the direction of the cranky bull. 'I guess the other option is to shoot him.'

'You can't shoot a healthy animal,' Hamish protested, and Harry shrugged.

'You want to try calming him down?' he said, nodding towards the trailer that had jackknifed and tipped onto its side in the middle of the road.

Kate walked towards it, seeing the tear in the top that had allowed Harry to check for dead or injured animals. A huge head, grey-black, with curved horns and, below them, floppy grey ears looked back at her. Somehow, the animal had managed to turn himself so he was upright, stamping and bellowing with either pain or frustration.

Knowing there was no way he could get out, she moved closer, talking softly to him, but he refused to be placated and kept up his complaints, his roars an accompaniment to the awful screeches of tearing metal.

'We're in, Doc,' one of the men called, and Kate left the irate bull to follow Hamish to the cabin.

Both its occupants, a man and a woman, were dead.

'It doesn't matter how often I see it, I hate the waste of life road accidents cause,' Hamish said, as he straightened after examining both bodies. 'Is the ambulance here?'

Kate nodded and waved the vehicle closer.

'It can take them into town. We'll do all the formalities at the hospital. I guess Harry will know who they are and who we need to contact.'

'It's Jenny and Brad Alcott,' one of the ambos said gruffly. 'They met on the rodeo circuit when they were young kids. Brad was a runaway who somehow hooked up with a rodeo stock contractor, and Jenny's mother ran a food van at rodeos for years. She died about six months ago from pancreatic cancer. These two nursed her to the end.'

After a fortnight in a country town, Kate was no longer surprised about how much people knew of each other's business, but she was saddened by the regret in the ambo's voice as he talked of the young couple.

'They were making a good job of providing quality rodeo

stock. Their Oscar is one of the best bulls on the northern circuit,' the man was saying to Hamish as they lifted the second body from the wreck. 'Dunno who'll take over from—'

He stopped abruptly, looked around, then said, 'Cripes, where's Lily?'

'Lily?' Hamish and Kate both echoed the name.

'Little 'un,' the ambo explained, holding out his hand to measure off about three feet from the ground. 'She was at the rodeo.'

Hamish and Kate looked at each other, but Kate was the first to move, scrabbling into the blood-covered seat from which they'd taken the adults, searching desperately through the twisted metal.

Although it hadn't been immediately obvious, the truck was a dual cab, with a second row of seats behind the front ones. Hamish pulled Kate out, explaining the crane would lift the damaged front seats out of the way.

'She might be alive. She might be injured and moving the seats will harm her.' Kate knew her anxiety was unprofessional, but the thought of a child trapped in the twisted mess of metal had her heart racing erratically.

The firemen hooked a chain to the less-damaged passenger seat and gave the signal for the crane to lift.

The little girl was curled in a foetal position in the footwell behind the seat, which had been tipped backwards on top of her. Blonde hair, a pink dress and blood. Blood everywhere.

Kate broke away from Hamish's restraining hand and knelt beside the child, talking quietly while her hand slid beneath the girl's chin, feeling for a pulse—praying for a pulse.

'Damn it, be alive!' she ordered, and felt not a pulse but a movement.

'She moved,' she cried, as Hamish squatted beside her, resting one hand on her shoulder while reaching out to touch the little girl's head, then sliding his hand down to the far side of her neck, seeking a pulse where Kate had found none.

It seemed to Kate that he took for ever, then one word. 'Pulse!'

Kate closed her eyes and uttered a little prayer of thanks. She wasn't certain anyone was listening to her prayers these days, but it didn't hurt to say thank you just in case.

'Lily!' Hamish's voice was gentle. 'Sweetheart, we're here to help you. My hand is on your back. Can you take a deep breath for me?'

Katie tensed as she waited, then Hamish nodded, shifting his hand so it followed the skinny little arm as it curled inwards.

'Now I've got your hand, sweetheart. Can you squeeze my hand?'

Another pause. 'Great!'

Kate heard the genuine delight in that one word.

'I can't reach your toes to tickle them,' Hamish continued, 'but can you wiggle them?'

The blonde head moved just slightly but it was definitely a nod, not a head shake.

'OK, so now we know we can move you a little bit. Do you want to lift your head up so Kate and I can look at you?'

This time it was definite head shake.

Kate, who'd been stroking the blood-matted hair, looked across at Hamish.

'There's a scalp wound here, above her right ear, that I think explains most of the visible blood, but if she was wearing her seat belt there could be soft-tissue damage to her chest or abdomen and even organ damage.'

'I wasn't wearing my seat belt. Mummy will be cross.'

The muffled words pierced Kate's heart, and she put her arms around the little curled-up ball of misery and gave her a hug.

'Maybe this is one case where not wearing a seat belt was lucky. Instead of flying through the windscreen, she's shot off the seat into that space,' Hamish said, sliding his arms down under the child so he could lift her out.

'Lily, we need to get you out of there so we can take a proper look at you. I'm going to lift you now, OK?'

No reply, but as Hamish lifted the little girl, she raised her head and looked at Kate, then put out her arms.

Kate nodded to Hamish and took the child, who attached herself like a limpet to Kate's chest.

'Do you think she knows?' Kate mouthed the words at Hamish above the little girl's head.

'Most probably,' Hamish muttered grimly. 'She's been there and conscious all the time and we've all been talking about things she shouldn't have heard.'

Kate rocked back and forth, holding Lily tightly, hoping human contact would help ease the shock and horror the little girl had suffered.

Hamish dressed the scalp wound, then continued his examination, hampered by the fact he could only work on the bits of Lily not clamped to Kate.

'She seems OK,' he said, shaking his head in disbelief that the child should have escaped unscathed—although it was only her physical self that had been lucky. Who knew what emotional toll losing both parents would take on her?

'That's Lily! She survived!' Harry approached, a rifle in one hand. He walked around Kate so he could see Lily's face—if she'd lift it from where it was burrowed into Kate's shoulder.

'Hey, Lily! It's Harry. How are you, little darling?'

The head lifted and while Hamish watched, Lily registered first the policeman, who was obviously a friend, and then the rifle in his hand.

'What are you going to shoot, Harry?' she asked, and Kate smiled at Hamish, sure this interest in Harry's job signalled the little girl was OK.

But it was Harry's response that surprised Hamish. The policeman frowned and looked around as if seeking something to distract the child. Then the bull, which had been mercifully silent since they'd found Lily, began to bellow again and the quiescent child who'd clung to Kate became a small tornado, kicking and fighting herself free of Kate's protective arms and dashing to the trailer.

'It's Oscar. You were going to shoot Oscar.'

She flung herself down on the torn trailer, so close to the huge head of the angry bull that Hamish reached out and lifted her away. She kicked and fought and screamed to be let down, while the bull became equally agitated.

'It's OK, Lily,' Hamish said, tightening his hold on the little girl, soothing and comforting her. 'Harry isn't going to shoot your bull, darling. No way! We won't let him.'

He handed her to Kate, who kissed her on the head and murmured, 'You stay here with me and talk to Oscar while Harry and Hamish work out how to get him out.'

'You've got to be kidding!' Hamish muttered, looking from Kate to the bull then back to Kate.

'You'll think of something,' Kate told him, hugging Lily closer to her body. 'Isn't there a vet? Couldn't you get a tran-quillising dart?'

'I tried to get the vet, but he's out on the Coopers' place, seeing to the cattle Charles wanted checked.' Harry sounded defensive. 'And don't think I like the idea of shooting a healthy animal, but you tell me what else we can do.'

'We have sedatives in our bags and the ambos will have more,' Kate said. 'We only have to do the sums. Hamish, how much do bulls weigh?'

'I'm Scottish,' Hamish protested. 'We have Highland cows but they're small, hairy, docile creatures and, believe me, I have no idea how much *they* weigh, let alone this guy.'

'Can't you work it out from people? I mean, a really big fat man might weigh, what? Three hundred pounds? Then you look at Oscar and work out how many big fat men it would take to make one of him—'

'You can't be serious!'

'You have any other ideas?' Kate demanded.

'Maybe it is the best way,' Harry said, cravenly giving in to Kate's persuasion.

'And we're going to give it to him how?' Hamish asked.

Harry shook his head but Kate turned her head to look at the bull, which appeared to be communing with Lily over Kate's shoulder.

'Intramuscularly, I'd say,' she told Hamish with a smile. 'I wouldn't like to mess around looking for a vein.'

Hamish shook his head again, but now a little smile was playing around his lips and Kate knew she'd won.

'I'll see what we have,' he said, then his smile grew. 'While you work out how to get it into him.'

'He seems a nice bull,' Kate said to Lily when the two men had departed.

'He's mine,' Lily told her. 'My very own. *And* we're friends.'

'I'm kind of glad about that,' Kate said, eyeing the extremely large animal, which looked as if he ate friends for breakfast. Except he did have soft brown eyes, and now she really looked, he had a friendly face.

'Does he let you pat him?'

'Of course he does,' Lily scoffed, reaching out a skinny arm towards the tear in the trailer.

'Be careful, you'll cut yourself,' Kate warned, but the little arm snaked inside and touched the bull's soft nose.

'Would he let me touch him?' Kate pursued.

Lily turned her head to look more closely at the woman to whom she still clung.

'If I told him to,' she said, without a hint of boasting or bravado in her voice.

'Well, when Dr Hamish gets the injection for him, will you tell Oscar to let me touch him? It's not going to hurt him, just put him to sleep for long enough for the men to cut him free and lift him into a truck.'

'Where will the truck take him?'

Lily's legs and arms tightened around Kate's body again and Kate knew the little girl must know, at some level where she didn't want to go, that her parents were dead.

'Wherever you say,' Kate told her, rocking her again.

'He has to come where I go,' Lily said, her voice breaking and warm tears spilling down Kate's neck. 'He has to stay with me. He's mine, he's mine.'

'He'll stay with you, darling, of course he will,' Kate promised, knowing the bond she felt with the child was more than sympathy for her loss, but an understanding of how total that loss must be. 'I promise you he'll stay.'

Hamish and Harry returned, Hamish holding a big bulb syringe Kate knew was normally used for irrigating ears.

'You have a needle on that thing?' Kate asked, and Hamish nodded proudly at her.

'Never let it be said a Scot can't improvise,' he said, showing her his invention, which had a hard plastic cannula attached to the blunt end of the syringe and a hollow hypodermic needle attached to the cannula. 'You ready?'

'Me?'

She may have talked to Lily about touching the big bull, but she hadn't for a minute imagined either Hamish or Harry would allow her to do it. Forget women's lib, this was a very large bull they were talking about.

But Hamish was offering her the syringe!

No chance. 'Lily, tell Oscar Hamish is a friend.'

The little girl, apparently unwilling to take Kate's word for it, wriggled around to look at Hamish.

'You're not going to hurt him, are you?'

Hamish smiled and touched her cheek.

'He'll hardly feel it,' he promised.

'Then I'll hold him.'

Still clinging with one arm to Kate, she stretched out the other and with an imperious 'Oscar, come!' she reached her hand into the damaged trailer.

The big bull stretched his neck, lowered his head and nuzzled her hand, allowing her to pat his nose then reach upward to grab hold of one of his horns.

'Stay!' Lily commanded, for all the world as if she were talking to a very obedient dog not an animal the size of a small elephant. Kate eyed the set-up. If the bull moved his head, he could tear off Lily's arm.

'I'll hold him, too,' she said, and shifted Lily to one hip.

'You'll stay right out of it!' Hamish ordered, placing his body between her and the bull and reaching in to grasp the thick horn above where Lily's small hand lay.

Then he took the chance, reaching in with his right hand and jabbing the needle into the bull's neck, then squeezing the bulb hard and fast to inject as much of the sedative as he could while Oscar remained still.

'It's not going to work,' Kate said ten minutes later, as all four of them watched the bull watching them through the tear in the trailer.

'He looks sleepy,' Lily told her. 'Soon he'll lie down.'

And within moments she was proved correct. The big animal started looking confused, then shook his head, before his legs gave way and he sank down onto what was now the base of the trailer.

The firemen moved in immediately, cutting through the metal shell then calling the tow truck closer and wrapping ropes around the inert body.

'Where am I taking him?' the truck driver asked, when Oscar was settled into the back of a cattle truck.

'To the hospital,' Kate answered, and all the men involved in the rescue turned to stare at her.

'He'll be OK when he comes round,' Hamish assured her,

his voice the kindly one he probably used to people who were off the planet.

'He needs to stay with Lily,' Kate explained, resting her head against the head of the now dozing child. 'Or she needs him to stay with her. And we have to take her to the hospital to check her out and contact relatives. There's that paddock at the back of the Agnes Wetherby Garden—I asked Charles about it one day and he said in the old days the hospital had its own cows. Oscar can go into the cow paddock.'

Harry shrugged and turned to the driver.

'You heard the lady,' he said, while Hamish came over and gave her and Lily a hug.

'And how long did it take you to work out all of that?' he asked, his arm around the pair of them, leading them away from the damaged trailer then stopping abruptly within sight of the ambulance.

Kate shifted Lily so the little girl's weight was on her hip and smiled at Hamish.

'You'd have worked it out just as quickly if you'd heard Lily talk about her bull,' Kate replied, then she checked to make sure the little one was still sleeping. 'She's lost so much, Hamish. How could we not keep her bull close to her?'

He hugged her again and she realised it wasn't just shoulder shrugs and kisses she'd miss. She'd miss Hamish's hugs…

But he wasn't thinking about hugs. Or, if he was, they weren't happy thoughts for he was frowning and looking around as if he'd lost something. Then he turned her and Lily round again and walked back towards the accident.

'Wait here a moment,' he said, sounding so definite Kate didn't argue, though Lily was growing ever heavier in her arms.

He returned, this time with Harry.

'I'll send you back in the second police car,' Harry said, and Kate, glancing back towards the ambulance that was to have been their transport, looked at Hamish and understood. He hadn't wanted Lily travelling with the vehicle that held her parents' bodies.

This was the Hamish that got under her defences. He might joke and make light of things most of the time, but underneath his detached exterior there was a heart that felt the pain of others and a steely determination to do whatever was possible to alleviate it.

'You'll go straight to the hospital?' Harry asked.

'Yes, we need to check her out and the staff there can start a search for relations,' Hamish told him.

'Good luck with that,' Harry said, still frowning, though Hamish felt the frown was directed at him, not at the task that lay ahead of them. 'Brad was a runaway and although a whole crowd of locals and rodeo folk turned out for Jenny's mother's funeral, I don't know that any of them were relatives.'

'We'll do our best, and in the meantime there are plenty of people at the hospital who can keep an eye on Lily.' Hamish wasn't sure why he was getting such negative vibes from Harry, who was usually an extremely positive person. Though maybe having to deal with two dead people and an untold number of dead animals might destroy anyone's positivity.

'So, tomorrow?'

It took a moment for Hamish to realise the question hadn't been directed at him. And that Kate was already answering it!

'I don't know,' she was saying hesitantly, looking down at the blonde head on her shoulder. 'I'll stay with Lily while ever she needs me. I'll let you know.'

Harry gave Hamish another disgruntled look and walked away.

'You were going out with him tomorrow?' Hamish demanded of Kate the moment the policeman was out of earshot.

'He was going to take me out on the river,' she said, 'but now…'

They were in the middle of the highway—mercifully still closed to traffic—halfway between the wrecked vehicles and the second police car, but Hamish wasn't moving another step until he'd sorted this out.

'Take you out on the river? I've asked you to dinner at Athina's, to a beach barbeque, to the movies and to the Black Cockatoo for a drink, and every single time you've given me the same excuse—you don't want to get involved. Yet you had a drink with Harry at the pub on Wednesday and now a second date?'

Somewhere deep inside him a voice Hamish didn't recognise was suggesting he was making a fool of himself—that maybe the woman just didn't like him, or liked Harry better. But he was sure the voice was wrong about her not liking him. Hadn't she kissed him—or at least returned his kisses—just that afternoon?

Could she like Harry better?

The voice was interrupting her reply so he ignored it for a moment to listen to whatever lame excuse she was about to offer.

'I know I keep having second thoughts about finding my father, but Harry's lived here all his life and must know everyone, and I thought maybe I'd find out from him if my father *does* have a family, and what they're like, and then maybe I could judge if I should make contact or not.'

'You're going out with him so you can find your father?'

The internal voice seemed to think that would be OK, except...

'Is that fair?''

'No, probably not!' Kate snapped at him, but Hamish, caught in the grip of an emotion he'd never felt before, couldn't let it go.

'So don't go out with him. Visit him at the police station. Ask him there. Make it an official visit.'

'I don't want to make it an official visit. That's the whole point. I want to find out about him first. He mightn't even be here. He might never have been here. He might have been someone passing through, someone my mother met on holiday. Anyway, this isn't the time or place to be talking about this. We've got to get Lily back to hospital. What's more, whether I go out with Harry or not is really none of your business!'

Stunned by her final statement, Hamish could only watch her back moving further and further away from him.

He'd lost her!

Not that he'd ever really had her—he'd just had hope, quite a lot of hope.

But he'd pushed too far. Now she'd go out with Harry just to spite him.

Or maybe not. He doubted there was a spiteful bone in Kate's body.

But the 'none of his business' phrase told him she was finished with whatever small flirtation she'd allowed herself to enjoy.

Pain he didn't understand bit in again. How could this possibly have happened?

To him, who didn't do love?

Kate watched him as he slipped into the police car—not into the back where she and Lily sat, but into the front beside the driver.

She read his hurt in the slump of his usually straight shoulders and the way he turned his head to look out into the darkness of the rainforest through which the road ran.

And pain of knowing she'd hurt him swamped her heart.

She stroked the hair of the little girl who was sleeping safely strapped in but with her head resting on Kate's body.

What *was* she thinking? What was the hurt of love compared with the loss this child had suffered? How had she and Hamish got into personal stuff while this little girl needed all their attention?

But, no matter how much she felt for Lily, it didn't stop the regret clutching at her gut when she glanced at the man in front of her in the car.

CHAPTER TEN

'NORMAL SATURDAY NIGHT chaos,' Hamish remarked as they walked into the emergency department with Lily.

He sounded OK—but, then, he did the colleague thing so well it was hard to tell.

Grace was doing admissions. She looked at the little girl in Kate's arms and shook her head, news of the accident and its devastating results having reached the hospital well ahead of them.

'You'll get her processed faster if the two of you do it,' she said. 'I know you're off duty, both of you, but if you wouldn't mind?'

'I want to check her out anyway,' Hamish assured Grace. 'Have you got a spare cubicle we can use?'

Grace tapped her keyboard.

'Room Five. I'll let Charles know you're here. He's been trying to find some close relatives.'

Hamish rested his hand lightly on the small of Kate's back and steered her and her sleeping burden towards the small examination room. She liked the touch, but she'd seen him do it to strangers, men and women.

Once inside Kate slumped down into a chair, turning the little girl so she rested against her body.

'Do you have to wake her?' She looked up into Hamish's concerned blue eyes.

Concerned or hurt?

She didn't know, though probably concerned—this was work after all.

'You know I do,' he said quietly. 'Let's get her on the table and clean her up a bit and see what we can see.'

He bent to lift Lily, the movement bringing his head close to Kate's and bringing something else to her mind—a prescience—as if this was a snapshot of the future—herself, Hamish and a child…

How could that be?

Not possible!

She must have shivered because before he lifted Lily Hamish brushed his thumb against Kate's temple.

'She'll be OK,' he said softly, then, just as she was feeling thankful he hadn't read her thoughts, he added, 'Maybe we all will be.'

Maybe? There were far too many maybes in her life right now.

Lily woke as Hamish settled her on the table and looked around in panic,which subsided when Kate reached out to hold her hand and explain what was going on. The child's eyes, a clear, pale blue, searched further, then, as if remembering what she sought wouldn't be there, they closed, shutting her off from the world and the dreadful reality it held.

'How is she?'

Charles asked the question as he and Jill came into the room.

'Miraculously all right,' Hamish replied, but his voice was sombre and no one really needed the 'physically' which he added to the sentence.

He straightened from his examination.

'She should be kept overnight anyway,' he said, 'purely for observation.'

Kate wanted to protest—to say Lily could stay with her, that she could watch her during the night—but Charles was already agreeing, and Kate knew it was the right thing for the child.

'I'll stay with her,' she said instead. 'I'm off duty tomorrow. I can sleep then.'

Charles looked at her, the frown she often saw on his face only just held at bay by a slight smile.

'Were you always bringing home stray dogs as a child, or is it only stray humans you collect?'

'I lived in the inner city—no stray dogs. And Jack's no longer my stray, he's Megan's.'

Kate wasn't sure why Charles always made her feel slightly uncomfortable. Was it just the frown, or something more?

Whatever, she edged a little closer to the table where Lily lay—and where Hamish stood beside her.

'I think Kate's one of those rare people whose compassion is like an aura she carries with her,' Jill said, startling the subject of her observation. 'People bond with her without really knowing why.'

'I think it's just that I was there—for both Jack and Lily,' Kate protested, acutely embarrassed to think she might have an aura of any kind floating somewhere around her body. 'And I'm still the person with the day off tomorrow, so it won't hurt me to stay with Lily.'

She bent over the little girl, explaining that Hamish wanted to keep her in hospital.

'Is it because my head hurts?'

'You didn't tell me your head hurt,' Hamish said.

Charles wheeled out of the room, calling for an orderly to take the child through to Radiology.

'It just started now,' Lily told him, and fear for the girl welled in Kate's chest as she thought of a deadly haematoma building pressure inside the little girl's skull.

'I should have done a CT scan earlier,' Hamish said to Kate as they stood outside the doors of the radiology department and waited for a result. He looked as anguished as Kate felt.

'Why?' Kate demanded, the argument on the road forgot-

ten as she tried to reduce the load of guilt he was now carrying.
'She was obeying commands, talking, open-eyed, top marks
in all her GCS responses. As far as we know, she hadn't lost
consciousness and there was no palpable depressed fracture or
other sign of skull fracture.'

'She had the cut on her scalp.'

'It bled a lot, that's all. There wasn't even swelling.'

Reassuring Hamish was helping Kate's nerves, but she was
just as pleased as he was when Charles emerged to tell them
the CT scan was clear.

'Her head's hurting where the cut is, and where's her Kate?'
he added, smiling so warmly at Kate she wondered why she'd
ever worried about his liking her.

'I'll go into her,' she said, but before she did she turned to
Hamish and squeezed him gently on the arm. 'See!' she added
softly, but she knew he wasn't comforted. He'd continue cas-
tigating himself for some time, although he'd followed ED
rules to the letter in his examination and treatment of the little
girl.

Kate walked into the X-ray room but Hamish was in front
of her, lifting Lily in his arms and carrying her out, following
Charles through to the four-bed children's room.

Lily grew heavy in his arms, falling so deeply asleep she
didn't wake up as he laid her on the bed or protest as Kate
changed her into a pair of child-size hospital pyjamas.

Still anxious about the little girl, Hamish wrote an order for
half-hourly obs, then did the first himself.

'We know there's no bleeding inside her skull, and no
damage to her skull. It's exhaustion,' Charles told him. 'You
and Kate are showing signs of it as well. Go and get some
dinner. I'll sit with Lily until you get back.'

'You'll sit with her?'

The question slipped out before Hamish could prevent it, but
Charles seemed more amused than annoyed.

'I *can* sit with patients!' he said with mock humility. 'I know the way to do it!'

Then he sighed.

'Actually, it's personal as well. More in the feuding Wetherby family saga,' he said regretfully. 'Her grandmother was a cousin, but my father stopped speaking to that branch of the family before I was born. I knew about Lily's grandmother, and probably should have made more of an effort to contact her after my father died, but—'

'Families!' Kate said, and Hamish wondered if Charles heard the understanding in her voice.

Or knew her link with Lily was more than empathy.

He looked down at the pale face, thinking of how much the child had lost—of how much Kate had lost.

No wonder she didn't want to trust the love that had sprung up between them lest it be stripped away from her. Easier by far to deny it existed, or to pass it off as attraction...

Easier by far to push it away by going out with Harry!

So why did this understanding not make him feel better—not reduce the primal urge he felt to throttle Harry and carry Kate off, bodily if necessary, to his lair?

Or Scotland...

'Go!' Charles said, and Hamish touched Kate on the shoulder then steered her away.

'He's lonely, isn't he?' she asked, as they walked towards the dining room. 'I hadn't thought about it before, but you could hear it in his voice when he talked of the family feud.'

Hamish nodded, understanding—and not saying that he heard it in her voice, too.

Not saying anything at all as he thought about loneliness in all its many manifestations.

His own future loneliness not least among them...

No! That was not to be. Kate felt something for him, so somehow he had to battle through her resistance—somehow.

* * *

'Doctors' house meeting?' Kate joked as they walked into the dining room to find Cal, Gina, Emily, Grace and Susie all sitting at a table.

With Harry!

'Harry's found the missing bulls,' Gina told her, when Kate had helped herself to some roast beef and vegetables and joined them.

'Missing bulls? What missing bulls?' Hamish, who was pulling a chair out for her, asked. 'Don't tell me we've got to put more bulls in the cow paddock. Charles'll have a fit!'

The others laughed but it was Cal, not Harry, who took up the explanation.

'The Alcotts definitely had four bulls at the rodeo, but when you bravely liberated Oscar, he was the only animal in the trailer. Ergo, three missing bulls.'

'So?' Kate said, looking around the table. 'You all seem particularly happy about Harry finding these three. Why?'

'Because they're at Wygera,' Gina said, as if that totally explained the group's pleasure.

'Rob Wingererra, the uncle of one of the girls who died in the car accident some weeks back, travelled the rodeo circuit for years, and later on worked with rodeo stock animals.' Once again it was Cal telling her what she needed to know to connect the dots. 'He helped the Alcotts set up their business, but returned to Wygera recently because his mother isn't well.'

'So when he was talking to them at the rodeo, about the swimming pool and the kids being bored—' Gina took up the tale, her excitement almost palpable '—the Alcotts suggested they leave some bulls with Rob so he can get the kids interested not only in bull riding but in the care of rodeo stock. Isn't it marvellous?'

A young couple dead—two young people with names—Brad and Jenny. A little girl orphaned, a truck driver injured. Kate's mind flashed back to the nightmare horror of the scene, and pushed away her meal. She wasn't at the marvellous part yet.

Then she felt Hamish's hand on her knee, squeezing gently, and she knew he hadn't reached the marvellous goal either.

But his touch brought comfort—comfort she shouldn't be accepting—but she could no more have shifted that hand than she could have swallowed food.

'It will be another interest for the kids at Wygera, and a challenging one at that. At least equal to playing chicken in their old bombs of cars,' he said gently. 'Gina and Cal have been very involved with the community because of the pool, and can see how having the bulls to care for will help even more. I know it seems a funny kind of industry but apparently there's good money to be made in breeding and training rodeo stock, and Rob can manage the business for Lily for as long as is necessary—'

'And other members of the community can get involved.' Kate could see the reason for the smiles now.

The conversation continued around her but she wasn't thinking about bulls, but about how nice it was to have Hamish's hand resting on her knee.

Stupid, really. The last thing she should be feeling pleased about was contact with Hamish. For a start, she'd just told him that what she did was none of his business. And if she set that minor hurdle aside, there was the fact that in less than a week he'd be gone, and the closer she was drawn to him, the more she'd miss him when that day arrived.

'So, are we on for tomorrow?'

Hamish's fingers tightening their hold suggested Harry's question might have been for her, but she'd drifted so far away from the conversation it took her a few seconds to make sense of it.

Hadn't she already told Harry she wouldn't be free tomorrow?

The others were now watching her with interest. Could they know about Hamish's hand on her knee?

And could she say yes to Harry when Hamish had his hand on her knee, and she could feel the tension in it, the tension in the man beside her—the man she'd already hurt with careless words this evening?

'I'm sitting with Lily tonight so I won't get much sleep,' she said, her voice genuinely regretful because Harry was her best chance of finding out more about her father, although Harry wasn't asking her out to be helpful.

'We could go in the afternoon,' Harry pursued, but even though Hamish had now removed his hand, leaving a cold patch on her skin, she shook her head.

'No, Harry,' she said, as gently as she could, embarrassed that this conversation was taking place in front of others but needing to get it said. 'I don't think it's a good idea.'

He glanced from her to Hamish, then back to her again, and she wondered why she didn't feel shivers down her spine when Harry's cool grey eyes looked at her.

It had to be more than eye colour…

'OK!' he said easily, but she sensed he was hurt, an impression confirmed when he stood up and left the table without even a casual goodbye.

'He's a good bloke,' Grace said stiffly, then she too stood up and departed.

Following Harry, or hiding hurt Kate hadn't suspected?

'How's that for breaking up a party?' Hamish asked no one in particular, while Gina stacked dirty plates at one corner of the table.

'Grace has been in love with Harry for ages,' Emily said quietly. 'Unfortunately, until Kate arrived, he's never shown any particular interest in women—or not in any woman working at the hospital.'

'Poor Grace,' Gina said. 'Love can be the pits!'

But though her voice showed sympathy, the smile she shared with Emily showed two people, at least, who'd been there in the pits but had since clambered out—both now glowing, annoyingly for Kate, with the radiance of love.

'Gina's right,' Hamish said gloomily, now only he and Kate were left at the table. 'Love can be the pits!'

'It's not love,' Kate told him firmly. 'It can't possibly be love. We've known each other exactly two weeks—people don't fall in love in two weeks.'

He said nothing for a moment, then caught her eyes and held them.

'I have,' he said, so firmly she knew it was true. 'I know you don't want to hear it, Kate. I know you have so many other issues that you don't need to hear it. But I have to say it.'

He glanced around, then tried to make a joke of something that was obviously killing him.

'We're back at wrong time and wrong place, aren't we—me declaring my love in the hospital dining room?'

And it was this feeble attempt at a joke that hurt Kate most. It pierced her heart and left it oozing pain.

She searched for words to make things better, but couldn't find any. She could only shake her head, slowly and sadly, not knowing now if the utter sadness inside her was for herself or Hamish.

Perhaps for both of them.

She sighed and went for practicality.

'I can't eat. I'm going back to sit with Lily,' she said, pushing back her chair and standing up. 'Isn't Mike organising a fire at the beach? Shouldn't you be helping or at least on your way there?'

Hamish offered a smile so pathetic she wished he'd growled or yelled at her.

'That's tomorrow night,' he said, then the slightest of gleams returned to his dark eyes. 'You're off duty and, as it happens, so am I. It won't be a date, of course, but we'll be sure to see each other there.'

Kate felt the shiver grey eyes hadn't caused. The beach, a fire, night sky, wave music lapping at the shore…

She'd run away from all that last time—but hadn't run far enough.

Hamish was persistent. She'd pushed him away but the gleam and his words suggested he hadn't quite given up.

This time would Hamish leave her at the door?

Maybe she should have gone out on the river with Harry after all.

In the end, they both missed the fire.

It had started innocently enough, with Lily asking Kate where they were keeping Oscar's food.

Hamish, Kate and Lily, still in hospital pyjamas, were sitting on the cow paddock fence watching Oscar who, to Kate's eyes, seemed perfectly content eating grass.

Hamish had arrived not long after dawn and, once assured Lily's obs were perfect and that both she and Kate had slept most of the night, had whisked Kate off to breakfast in the dining room. They'd returned to the children's room to find Lily up and about, demanding to be taken to visit her friend.

So here they were.

'Food?' Kate repeated vaguely, her mind involved with whether she felt the effects of Hamish's presence more keenly in the morning or the afternoon. 'Isn't grass food?'

'No, silly, he needs his pellets.'

Kate had heard of pellets, but she rather thought it had been in connection with guns of some kind. Air rifles? Shotguns?

'Pellets?' Hamish repeated, saving Kate the embarrassment of mentioning firearms.

'Pellet food. It's at home,' Lily continued. 'We'll have to go and get some.'

The three of them had already had a number of conversations about Lily's missing parents but Kate wondered if the little girl really understood they were dead. Was this interest in Oscar's food an excuse to go to her place? Was she thinking her parents might be there?

And if so, would going there and not finding them make it harder or easier for her to accept their loss?

She glanced at Hamish over the child's head and read the same worries in his face and in the small shrug he gave.

'We'd better talk to Charles,' Kate said, surprising herself at how easily she'd fallen into the way of all the hospital staff who saw Charles as the solver of all puzzles large and small. Although if Charles was a relative…

'OK,' Lily said happily, climbing down from the fence and heading towards the hospital.

'How do you know where his office is?' Hamish asked, as Lily led them unerringly towards it.

'I talked to Charles and Jill this morning when you two were at breakfast,' Lily told her. 'He asked about my dad's family, if I had aunts and uncles, and I told him I didn't have any, but he's a kind of cousin and he says I can stay with him until something is sorted out.'

Lily paused in her forward progress and turned to Hamish.

'Charles knows a lot about bulls,' she confided. 'As well as a lot of other stuff. And Charles says there are plenty of people around the hospital who can take care of me when he's working. Do you know Mrs Grubb?'

Hamish smiled at the little girl.

'I do know Mrs Grubb,' he assured her, while Kate guessed the woman in question had already found her way to Lily's heart through chocolate-chip cookies.

But Charles?

Kate smiled to herself.

What could be more perfect—if Charles was lonely—than to have a lively little girl like Lily come into his life?

'Happy families?' Hamish murmured, reading Kate's thoughts again as Lily hurried ahead of them. 'Would it work?'

'It might,' Kate responded cautiously, hoping it would but knowing how ephemeral happiness could be.

Reaching the office, Lily wandered in as if she already belonged in the hospital family and greeted Charles like an equal. She then explained the food problem, far more succinctly than Kate could have.

'Ah!' Charles said, nodding and smiling at his new young friend. 'Did you explain to Kate and Hamish what the pellets are?'

'I told them they were Oscar's food,' Lily replied, and it was Charles who provided more information.

'Rodeo stock need special care. The owners work out exactly what they need and write out...a recipe, I suppose you'd call it, with the balance of protein, vitamins and minerals each particular animal requires, then stock-feed companies make it up into pellets. Oscar would be fed these in the morning and some hay when he's brought into his own pen in the afternoon. It's one of the reasons rodeo stock is easier to handle, because the animals *are* fed twice daily and are used to their handlers being around.'

Kate looked at him and shook her head, while Hamish appeared equally bemused.

'If Lily had a pet shark, would you know what to feed him as well?' Kate asked, remembering Daniel talking about some trendy friend who kept a shark in his living room.

Charles smiled at her.

'Fish, I would think,' he said, then turned his attention to Hamish.

'I'd go myself but there's a Health Department bigwig flying in this morning. Would you mind driving Lily out there? You can take the station wagon and pick up a couple of bags of the pellets. Eventually we'll get it all shifted to Wygera.'

'Can Kate come?' Lily asked, grasping Kate's hand.

Charles's eyes met Kate's above the blonde head, and Kate

knew he was thinking what she'd thought earlier—that maybe
Lily needed to see for herself that there was no one there.

And maybe when she saw that, she'd need someone to hold
her while she cried...

'Is it far?' Kate asked, all innocence.

'Oh, no,' Charles said. 'Two hundred—not much more.'

'Miles?' Kate said weakly.

And Hamish laughed.

'City girl!' he teased. 'Up here, it's what's known as a nice
Sunday drive. Isn't that right, Charles?'

It *was* a nice Sunday drive, but the togetherness of it disturbed Kate. Too many emotions mixed and intermingled—the
pleasure of being in a car with Hamish, the genuine joy she felt
in Lily's presence, the heart-breaking strength of Hamish as he
carried a very subdued little girl through her deserted home
then knelt with her, helping her choose toys and clothes for
Kate to pack. Singing silly songs as they drove home, until Lily
fell asleep in the back seat.

It was family yet not family.

It was something glimpsed then snatched away.

It was very, very confusing for a bruised and aching heart.

CHAPTER ELEVEN

THREE WEEKS AGO, Hamish had been looking forward to this dinner with Charles. It was to be Charles's private farewell to him, on the Tuesday night before Hamish's departure on the Friday.

But now…

'For a man returning home to the job of his dreams, you don't seem particularly happy,' Charles remarked, and Hamish, who was sure he'd been hiding his misery, shrugged his shoulders at the man who had become a friend.

'Kate?'

This time Hamish nodded, not wanting to talk about the woman with whom he'd so foolishly fallen in love.

'Well, it can't be that she doesn't love you,' Charles said, startling Hamish into speech.

'I beg your pardon?'

Charles smiled at him.

'I said it can't be that she doesn't love you. One only has to stand near her when you're around to feel the warmth of love radiating out of her body. Does she not want to go to Scotland? Has she reasons for wanting to stay in Australia? Perhaps she's afraid of starting a new life so far away from her family.'

'She doesn't have a family!' Hamish muttered crossly. 'That's the whole bloomin' trouble. Or I think it is. I think you're right about her at least liking me enough to give it a go, but she's been through so much…'

She'd kill him if he talked about her troubles—with a scalpel, he thought, or was that fate reserved for anyone who pitied her?

'Tell me.'

Two words, quietly spoken, but enough for Hamish to stop pretending to eat the delicious stuffed vine leaves he'd ordered for dinner and forget death by scalpel. He poured out the whole story into Charles's receptive ears.

'So she came up here to find her father?'

Charles had somehow found the main issue in the muddled tale Hamish had told.

'Has she found him?'

Hamish looked at his friend, Kate and her problems for once relegated to a position of lesser importance in his mind. Charles was sounding stressed and anxious. He'd been through some tough emotional crises recently—could they have affected his health?

'Has she?'

The abrupt demand brought Hamish back to the conversation in hand, though he'd speak to Cal about Charles's health as soon as he got back to the house.

'Well, no,' Hamish admitted. 'I think the shock of finding out she was fostered and then losing her rat of a fiancé propelled her into immediate action. She tracked down her mother first, but she had died. People in the place where her mother had lived mentioned Crocodile Creek. Kate was running on emotion and it wasn't until she arrived here that she realised a twenty-seven-year-old daughter might not be quite what her father wanted in his life. All the what ifs surfaced in her head.'

'She's twenty-seven? When is her birthday?'

Hamish was sure this was the least important part of the conversation he'd had with Charles, but he was now seriously enough worried about the man to go along with it.

'August. I only know because her birthday is the same day as Lucky's.'

'Of course it would be,' Charles muttered, making so little sense Hamish wondered about a stroke, although the words were clearly enunciated. 'What's her mother's name? Has she told you?'

Hamish tried to remember, then shook his head.

'But I've seen a photo. She was going to show it to Harry because he's lived here for ever, then she got cold feet about it all, but she showed it to me.' Hamish paused, still concerned about his dinner companion, but as Charles wasn't showing any symptoms of imminent collapse, he continued. 'Mind you, she doesn't really need the photo. She's the dead ringer for her mother.'

'Two years in the country and you're talking like a native,' Charles said, pushing his half-eaten dinner away and wheeling back from the table. 'Come on, we're getting out of here.'

He waved to Sophia Poulos, who was used to hospital staff leaving halfway through their meals, apologised when she came over and asked her to put the bill on his tab, then led Hamish out of the restaurant, down the ramp and out to his specially modified vehicle.

Hamish kept his mouth shut, although the questions he wanted to ask were clamouring to escape.

'Kate at home?' was all Charles said, as they drove back across the bridge, past the hospital and up to the house.

'She's not on duty,' Hamish managed to admit, although he was becoming more and more disturbed by Charles's behaviour.

'Good! See if you can find her, would you, and ask her to see me in the downstairs lounge. You'd better come, too. Might come as a shock to her to learn I'm her father.'

'*What?* You? Oh, come on, Charles! You can't know that! You don't even know her mother's name—'

'Oh, yes, I do!' Charles snapped. 'It was Maryanne, all one word, no hyphen. And she was, as you said, a dead ringer for Kate, only you said it the other way around.'

Hamish struggled to absorb this information, and struggled even more with his reaction to it. Loving Kate as he did, surely he should be glad for her if Charles did turn out to be her father. Charles, in fact, would be the perfect choice. No wife or children to cause awkwardness, a loving man who would take Kate into his heart without reservation and give her all the love and security she so badly needed.

But to Hamish it was the death of his last hope—the one that if Kate decided not to worry about finding her father she might give in to his pleas and join him in marriage, making a family of their own.

'I'll see if I can find her,' he told Charles, 'though I hardly think that room downstairs is the right place for this conversation. There are sure to be some of the staff down there, and Kate's a very private person.'

'The garden, then,' Charles suggested, as the hoist on his car lowered his wheelchair. 'Kate's told me how much she loves the garden, so she'll feel at ease there.'

I always seem to be waking her up, Hamish thought as he stood in the doorway of Kate's bedroom and looked at her sleeping figure. It was only ten, but she'd been on duty at six, then had played with Lily when she'd finished work.

Hamish sighed, knowing he had to wake her—knowing for her this might be the most wonderful news in the world.

Knowing it was going to break his heart.

But he couldn't yell from the door—everyone in the house would wonder what was going on—so he went quietly into the bedroom, saying her name as he did so, coming to the bed and bending to touch her shoulder.

'Kate, it's Hamish.'

She woke as quickly as most medical staff did, used to

being on call. She sat straight up, the hippo stretching out across her breasts.

'Hamish?'

Her voice was muddled with sleep, but full of…well, affection at least, though to Hamish it sounded like love.

'It's OK,' he said gently, sitting down on the bed and putting his arms around her. 'I'm sorry to wake you but Charles wants to talk to you.'

'Is it Lily?'

He tightened his arms around her when he heard the panic in her voice and reminded her that Lily was sleeping over with CJ, reassuring her Lily was just fine.

'But Charles? Me? What time is it?'

A lot less love or affection now, and who could blame her, considering the broken nights' sleep she'd been having lately?

'Just gone ten. He's in the garden. It's important, love.'

'It had better be,' his love snapped, shrugging away from his embrace so she could get out of bed. 'It had bloody well better be! Jack's OK, Lily's OK, I was looking forward to the first good night's sleep I've had since I arrived in this place.'

She was pulling on her sweatpants as she grumbled, then she ran a brush through her hair, slipped her feet into sandals—this time pink ones with a rose between the toes—and left the room.

Once again, though cravenly this time, Hamish wanted nothing more than to slide between her body-warmed sheets and stay there at least until morning—possibly until he had to leave Australia.

But he followed her out of the house, catching up with her on the back steps.

'What on earth's this about?' she demanded, slightly less aggrieved now.

'It's personal,' he said, slipping an arm around her shoulders and holding her close.

Wrong move. She stopped abruptly and turned towards him, and though it was dark he could see the flare of anger in her eyes.

'Personal? How? Don't tell me you asked him to intercede on your behalf? Asked him to talk to me about going to Scotland with you? *And* woke me up!'

Then she answered her own questions with a decisive shake of her head.

'No, you wouldn't do that. I'm sorry. But personal?'

'It's about your family.' Hamish made the admission reluctantly, knowing the anger she'd just quenched could so easily flare again. 'I'm sorry, I didn't intend to tell him anything, but he wanted to know why you wouldn't consider coming back to Scotland with me and somehow the bit about looking for your father came out.'

But Kate's only response was a sigh, then she lifted her hand and touched his cheek.

'What a mess of a person you got involved with,' she said quietly.

He forgot about Charles waiting in the garden and the bizarre turn events had taken, and took her in his arms and kissed her.

Though sure she was strong enough to handle Charles's revelation on her own, Hamish went with her. This was personal—between her and Charles—but he wasn't going to let go just yet.

Charles was waiting by the garden seat and Hamish could see his tension in the way white-knuckled hands gripped the wheels of his chair.

Maybe he should stay for Charles...

'Kate!'

Charles said her name and nodded to the garden seat. Hamish guided her towards it, sitting her down but keeping his arm firmly fixed around her shoulders, though Charles reached out to take both her hands in his.

'I don't know where to start, my dear, but when Hamish told me—'

He broke off and turned to Hamish, who knew full well he shouldn't be there—yet Charles seemed to need support now as much as Kate would later.

'Charles thinks…' Hamish paused then saw Charles nod for him to continue. 'He thinks he knew your mother.'

Kate stiffened in his arms and her lips moved, but no words came out so Hamish tucked her closer and dug deeper into his heart, trying to find a way to help two people he loved over such an awesome emotional hurdle.

'He knew and loved—' he'd bloody better have loved her, a savage voice muttered in his head '—a young woman who looked so much like you, you've been like a ghost walking through his life since you arrived.'

Hamish used his free hand to tilt Kate's chin so he could look into her eyes.

'Her name was—'

'Maryanne!'

Charles choked out the word then lifted Kate's hands in his, waiting, waiting, until finally a nod—so small if might have passed unnoticed if she hadn't at the same time begun to cry.

'My dear! Kate!' Charles raised her hands to his lips and pressed kisses on them, before looking up at her, his face whitely gaunt as he added, 'Am I right?'

Kate nodded again, more firmly this time, then dropped her head to rest on their clasped hands.

Hamish waited until Charles began to stroke the soft brown curls, then he stood up and moved quietly away.

He'd not go far—Kate might need him later—but right now these two people needed just to be together.

Hamish was dozing, his head against the iron lace that decorated the balustrade on the staircase, when Charles brought her back, stopping at the bottom of the steps and holding tightly to both Kate's hands.

Later, Kate knew, they would need to talk some more, but right now, in the early hours of the morning, they were both too overwhelmed by a multitude of emotions to do anything but cling to each other.

'You need some sleep,' Charles told her gruffly, and she bent and kissed his cheek.

'So do you,' she whispered, then she nodded to her sleeping guard. 'And so does Hamish.'

Charles released her hands and backed away so he could turn to go back to his car. Light from the house glinted on the wheels of his chair, and picked up the faint sheen of moisture on his cheeks.

Kate waited until he was no longer in sight, then she touched Hamish lightly on the head.

'Hey! You should be in bed,' she said, but instead of continuing on up the steps she sat down beside him, knowing he'd put his arm around her—needing the solidity and comfort of it.

He didn't say anything immediately, which was just as well because she was having trouble sorting it all out in her head, but when he finally said 'Well?' the words came tumbling out—the story of a young woman who had been working out at Wetherby Downs and a young man home from boarding school, barely a man at seventeen but man enough to fall in love.

'He went back to school at the end of January, promising to keep in touch. They were so in love they'd already talked of marriage when he finished school and returned to the property at the end of the year. He wrote and she replied, until the week before the Easter break. When he didn't get an answer he phoned home, to be told Maryanne had left. He flew home in the mid-year break and contacted Maryanne's aunt, who'd brought her up in Crocodile Creek, but the aunt thought she was still at Wetherby Downs. He asked around, but she'd vanished as completely as if she'd never been.'

'Charles's father, from all I've heard, was a terrible man,' Hamish said quietly. 'No doubt if he thought she posed a threat to his plans for his son, she'd have had to go. By Easter, the old man would probably have known or guessed that she was pregnant.'

Kate nodded against his shoulder, too overwhelmed by emotion to say any more. Although, somewhere in her head she was wondering why she wasn't happier. Why finding her father—knowing she had family—hadn't brought the joy and ease and peace she'd thought it would?

'Walk on the headland?'

Hamish's suggestion eased a lot of her tension. Knowing she wouldn't be able to sleep, she'd been dreading going back to her lonely room. But Hamish should be sleeping—they were both on duty in the morning—there was no reason she should keep him up.

'Come on,' he said, easing away from her to stand up and pull her up after him. 'I could use the walk myself.'

But walking on the headland where she and Hamish had first kissed was not a good idea. Sure, she'd almost managed to put Charles's revelations out of her head, but now she was far too conscious of Hamish—of the feel of his bones beneath the flesh of his fingers, of the warmth of the muscles beneath the skin of his thighs. Bits of Hamish she'd never even considered seemed to be calling to her, tempting her, pulling her towards him, so when he stopped at the highest point where the sea broke against the cliff beneath them, she turned into his arms and lifted her head for his kiss.

And what happened to not kissing Hamish any more? her conscience demanded.

Tonight's different, she reminded it, although she knew that was just an excuse. No matter what had happened, she shouldn't, definitely shouldn't, be kissing Hamish!

The pressure of his lips opened hers, and she tasted his uniqueness, tart yet sweet—addictive, as addictive as the feel of his body against hers and the strength of the arms that held her close. As addictive as the softly accented words he whispered in her ear, and the way his fingers caught a curl and twirled it round and round.

She sighed and he caught the sound in his mouth and turned it back to her, then the intoxication of the kisses took over and she stopped thinking, simply responding with her lips and hands, exploring more and more of him, knowing she needed to know him with every sense so she could keep the memory for ever.

'I love this place. I could stay—*not* go back,' he said quietly, when, sated with kisses, they walked again.

And knowing just how much the position in the paediatrics team meant to him, Kate understood the magnitude of the offer he was making.

She turned and put her arms around him, resting her head on his chest.

'Oh, Hamish! That's the sweetest, kindest, most wonderful thing you could ever have said to me, but it's not a matter of geography. I know, having just found Charles, that leaving him would be very hard to do, but there are phones and emails and even planes that fly from here to there and back again. So…'

Knowing she needed words as she'd never needed them before, she searched her tired, over-excited mind.

But how to explain?

'It's love that worries me,' she said in the end. 'And all that love entails. The giving over so completely of oneself, the responsibility for someone else's happiness—it frightens me too much, Hamish. Yes, it's magic when it works—the magic that you've talked of, a precious magic. But when it doesn't?'

She moved away from him but he drew her back, holding her in his arms as if he'd never let her go.

'It's love,' she whispered again, hating the word that was paining her so much. 'Love's—love's so full of hurt!'

And she pressed her face against his shirt and wrapped her arms around him.

They stood like that for a while, until he moved so they were side by side again. Then arm in arm, with saddened, heavy hearts, they walked back towards the old house.

Kate leaned against the gate of the cow paddock, watching Lily as she sat on the lush lawn inside the fence, pulling up handfuls of grass and feeding them to Oscar, chatting all the time, telling him she was going to live with Charles and that he'd be going to Wygera with the other bulls but Charles would take her to visit him often.

The gentle giant stood in front of her, carefully lipping the offerings from her small hand, a look of bemused benevolence on his face.

Kate felt Hamish's presence a moment before he joined her, folding his arms on the top rail and resting his chin on them so he, too, could watch the pair.

He'd asked her so often to go back to Scotland with him but Kate knew that today—the day before he left—he wouldn't ask again.

It was up to her.

She slid a glance towards him—saw the strong, angular planes of his face, the almost arrogant masculinity of this gentle, caring man, and her heart all but seized up when she considered never seeing him again…

'It's all about trust, isn't it?' she said, nodding towards the pair in the paddock. 'By trusting Oscar, she's virtually handed him her life, hasn't she?'

'It is, and she has,' Hamish replied, and the depth of emotion in his voice told Kate he knew she wasn't talking about Lily and the bull. 'But she's young,' he continued. 'She's never had reason to lose trust—never had it betrayed.'

Kate turned and looked properly at him, seeing the face she loved so dearly strained and tired.

'But she lost her parents,' she said, needing to argue with him no matter how tired he looked.

'Death isn't a betrayal,' Hamish reminded her. 'And it shouldn't be seen that way.'

'It wasn't my parents' deaths but that they hadn't told me,' Kate whispered, and Hamish took her in his arms and held her close.

'Do you think I don't know that, Kateling? Do you think I can't feel your hurt or understand your unwillingness to trust again? I can and I do, but I can't make you trust me. Trust's something that has to be given freely or it's a worthless gift.'

Kate looked up into the anguished eyes above her, then she rose on tiptoe and kissed him on the chin.

'Will you take my trust?' she murmured, and watched his anguish change to puzzlement then to something that looked like a very cautious hope.

'Are you offering it?' he asked, his voice harshly raspy with emotion.

Kate tried a tentative smile, and took a deep gulp of air.

'I am,' she said, and waited.

And waited.

Then Hamish gave a whoop that startled Oscar into skittishness and had Lily scolding both of them for giving her a fright.

'You mean it? You'll marry me?'

'I do and I will,' Kate said, her voice shaking so much she just hoped the words were distinguishable.

They must have been for Hamish's grasp tightened, but belief, she realised, was still a little way off.

'And Charles? Your family here? You do realise you have

family, don't you? Beyond Charles, you and Jack are cousins. You and Lily are related.'

'Charles said he'll bring Lily to visit us. Jack and Megan and Jackson can come, too. I thought we might give Jack and Megan money for their fares as a wedding present. Then when you've finished your paediatric training…'

'We'll come back here?' The words were hushed with disbelief, as if the last thing Hamish had been expecting was a miracle.

But something must have sunk in for he released her suddenly, stepping back and peering suspiciously down into her face.

'Whoa! Back up here,' he said sternly. 'Charles said he'll come and visit? He'll bring Lily? How come Charles knows where you'll be to visit, before you got around to telling me?'

Hamish watched the colour rise in her cheeks and wondered if he'd ever tire of looking at this woman. She raised those soft brown eyes, now brimming with embarrassment, then offered an equally embarrassed smile.

'Everyone knows Charles knows everything,' she teased, and though it was a brave try, Hamish refused to let her get away with it.

He raised his eyebrows and waited.

And waited.

'Charles had a long talk to me this morning,' Kate finally explained, then she swallowed hard and for a moment Hamish regretted pushing her. In fact, he wanted to take her in his arms and keep her there for ever, no matter how this miracle had happened.

But before he could do anything, she was speaking again.

'He talked to me about my birth mother, not who she was and what had happened between them—he'd told me all of that before. But this morning he told me how much he'd loved her and how much he's always regretted not going after her—not searching for her until he found her.'

Kate blinked but not before one tear had escaped, to roll slowly down her flushed cheek.

'He said regret was a terrible companion with whom to spend your life, but even worse was the knowledge that he'd once been offered the very precious gift of love and he hadn't grasped it with both hands. That, he said, was stupidity, and he hoped like hell he hadn't passed on the stupid gene to his daughter.'

Now more tears were following the first, hurting Hamish's heart just to look at them. He pulled her close and held her tightly, using her body to anchor his to the ground as the realisation that she was his for ever filled him with a heady, dizzying delight.

'I love you,' he managed to whisper gruffly, knowing the words needed to be said.

'And I love you,' Kate responded, drawing away from his embrace so she could look into his eyes. 'With all my heart!' she added.

Then she kissed him again, while across the fence Oscar nodded benevolently.

Everyone was there—Christina and Joe, back from New Zealand with Joe's mother and sister in tow, Emily and Mike, Cal and Gina, CJ and Rudolph. Grace was there, and Susie, Georgie and young Max, and Jill, standing quietly next to Charles, who held Lily on his lap—all lining the drive between the house and the hospital—all yelling good luck and best wishes and waving streamers.

The old house that had seen so much now saw them go—a certain warmth departing with them. But it had stood too long to think love wouldn't bloom again within its walls.

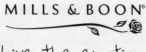

MILLS & BOON®

Live the emotion

APRIL 2006 HARDBACK TITLES

ROMANCE™

Prince of the Desert *Penny Jordan*	H6356	0 263 19150 8
For Pleasure...Or Marriage? *Julia James*	H6357	0 263 19151 6
The Italian's Price *Diana Hamilton*	H6358	0 263 19152 4
The Jet-Set Seduction *Sandra Field*	H6359	0 263 19153 2
His Private Mistress *Chantelle Shaw*	H6360	0 263 19154 0
Bertoluzzi's Heiress Bride *Catherine Spencer*		
	H6361	0 263 19155 9
Captive in His Bed *Sandra Marton*	H6362	0 263 19156 7
Kept by the Tycoon *Lee Wilkinson*	H6363	0 263 19157 5
Her Outback Protector *Margaret Way*	H6364	0 263 19158 3
The Sheikh's Secret *Barbara McMahon*	H6365	0 263 19159 1
A Woman Worth Loving *Jackie Braun*	H6366	0 263 19160 5
Her Ready-Made Family *Jessica Hart*	H6367	0 263 19161 3
The Nanny Solution *Susan Meier*	H6368	0 263 19162 1
A Taste of Paradise *Patricia Thayer*	H6369	0 263 19163 X
Maternal Instinct *Caroline Anderson*	H6370	0 263 19164 8
The Doctor's Proposal *Marion Lennox*	H6371	0 263 19165 6

HISTORICAL ROMANCE™

The Rogue's Kiss *Emily Bascom*	H630	0 263 19039 0
A Treacherous Proposition *Patricia Frances Rowell*		
	H631	0 263 19040 4
Rowan's Revenge *June Francis*	H632	0 263 19041 2

MEDICAL ROMANCE™

The Doctor's Marriage Wish *Meredith Webber*		
	M539	0 263 19084 6
The Surgeon's Perfect Match *Alison Roberts*		
	M540	0 263 19085 4

0306 Gen Std HB

MILLS & BOON®

Live the emotion

APRIL 2006 LARGE PRINT TITLES

ROMANCE™

Blackmailing the Society Bride *Penny Jordan*
1855   0 263 18958 9
Baby of Shame *Julia James*   1856   0 263 18959 7
Taken by the Highest Bidder *Jane Porter*   1857   0 263 18960 0
Virgin for Sale *Susan Stephens*   1858   0 263 18961 9
A Most Suitable Wife *Jessica Steele*   1859   0 263 18962 7
In the Arms of the Sheikh *Sophie Weston*
1860   0 263 18963 5
The Marriage Miracle *Liz Fielding*   1861   0 263 18964 3
Ordinary Girl, Society Groom *Natasha Oakley*
1862   0 263 18965 1

HISTORICAL ROMANCE™

The Outrageous Debutante *Anne O'Brien*   328   0 263 18905 8
The Captain's Lady *Margaret McPhee*   329   0 263 18906 6
Winter Woman *Jenna Kernan*   330   0 263 19069 2

MEDICAL ROMANCE™

Bride by Accident *Marion Lennox*   601   0 263 18863 9
Coming Home to Katoomba *Lucy Clark*   602   0 263 18864 7
The Consultant's Special Rescue *Joanna Neil*
603   0 263 18865 5
The Heroic Surgeon *Olivia Gates*   604   0 263 18866 3

0306 Gen Std LP

MILLS & BOON®

Live the emotion

MAY 2006 HARDBACK TITLES

ROMANCE™

The Secret Baby Revenge *Emma Darcy*	H6372	0 263 19166 4
The Prince's Virgin Wife *Lucy Monroe*	H6373	0 263 19167 2
Taken for His Pleasure *Carol Marinelli*	H6374	0 263 19168 0
At the Greek Tycoon's Bidding *Cathy Williams*		
	H6375	0 263 19169 9
The Mediterranean Millionaire's Mistress *Maggie Cox*		
	H6376	0 263 19170 2
By Royal Demand *Robyn Donald*		
	H6377	0 263 19171 0
In the Venetian's Bed *Susan Stephens*	H6378	0 263 19172 9
A Forbidden Passion *Carla Cassidy*	H6379	0 263 19173 7
The Heir's Chosen Bride *Marion Lennox*	H6380	0 263 19174 5
The Millionaire's Cinderella Wife *Lilian Darcy*		
	H6381	0 263 19175 3
Their Unfinished Business *Jackie Braun*	H6382	0 263 19176 1
The Tycoon's Proposal *Leigh Michaels*	H6383	0 263 19177 X
The Virgin's Proposal *Shirley Jump*	H6384	0 263 19178 8
Finding a Family *Judy Christenberry*	H6385	0 263 19179 6
A Baby of His Own *Jennifer Taylor*	H6386	0 263 19180 X
A Nurse Worth Waiting For *Gill Sanderson*	H6387	0 263 19181 8

HISTORICAL ROMANCE™

The Viscount's Betrothal *Louise Allen*	H633	0 263 19042 0
Reforming the Rake *Sarah Elliott*	H634	0 263 19043 9
Lord Greville's Captive *Nicola Cornick*	H635	0 263 19044 7

MEDICAL ROMANCE™

The Midwife's Special Delivery *Carol Marinelli*		
	M541	0 263 19086 2
Emergency In Alaska *Dianne Drake*	M542	0 263 19087 0

0406 Gen Std HB

MILLS & BOON®

Live the emotion

MAY 2006 LARGE PRINT TITLES

ROMANCE™

The Sheikh's Innocent Bride *Lynne Graham*
1863 0 263 18966 X

Bought by the Greek Tycoon *Jacqueline Baird*
1864 0 263 18967 8

The Count's Blackmail Bargain *Sara Craven*
1865 0 263 18968 6

The Italian Millionaire's Virgin Wife *Diana Hamilton*
1866 0 263 18969 4

Her Italian Boss's Agenda *Lucy Gordon*   1867 0 263 18970 8

A Bride Worth Waiting For *Caroline Anderson*
1868 0 263 18971 6

A Father in the Making *Ally Blake*   1869 0 263 18972 4

The Wedding Surprise *Trish Wylie*   1870 0 263 18973 2

HISTORICAL ROMANCE™

The Venetian's Mistress *Ann Elizabeth Cree*
331 0 263 18907 4

Bachelor Duke *Mary Nichols*   332 0 263 18908 2

The Knave and the Maiden *Blythe Gifford*   333 0 263 19070 6

MEDICAL ROMANCE™

The Nurse's Christmas Wish *Sarah Morgan* 605 0 263 18867 1

The Consultant's Christmas Proposal *Kate Hardy*
606 0 263 18868 X

Nurse In a Million *Jennifer Taylor*   607 0 263 18869 8

A Child To Call Her Own *Gill Sanderson*   608 0 263 18870 7

0406 Gen Std LP